"Just how badly," Trevor said, "do you wish me to stay?"

"I've told you how important Blackcliff is to the village, sir."

"Indeed. The last lifeblood it seems. You've gone to great lengths to prove to me how well I'll like it here. Are you setting me a mystery to sweeten the pie?"

A mystery? Gwen had been right—some part of him relished this challenge with the statue.

"I have no part in this, Trevor. Or do you think I'm the one moving the statue?"

"The idea had crossed my mind."

For some reason, the accusation hurt. "Do you truly think me so devious?"

"Not devious," he replied. "But determined. You admit you'd do anything to make me stay," he said.

"I admit I wanted you to stay," Gwen replied, "but this presumptuous attitude is not endearing you to me, sir."

"Forgive me, Gwen. I should know there's no guile in you. You have been nothing but kindness itself to me since the day I arrived."

Well, that was better. She could only hope that he truly had decided she was innocent. And that maybe, maybe, this puzzle would give him a reason to stay for a while longer.

Books by Regina Scott

Love Inspired Historical

The Irresistible Earl
An Honorable Gentleman

REGINA SCOTT

started writing novels in the third grade. Thankfully for literature as we know it, she didn't actually sell her first novel until she had learned a bit more about writing. Since her first book was published in 1998, her stories have traveled the globe, with translations in many languages including Dutch, German, Italian and Portuguese.

She and her husband of more than twenty years reside in southeast Washington state. Regina Scott is a decent fencer, owns a historical costume collection that takes up over a third of her large closet and she is an active member of the Church of the Nazarene. Her friends and church family know that if you want something organized, you call Regina. You can find her online blogging at www.nineteenteen.blogspot.com. Learn more about her at www.reginascott.com.

An Honorable Gentleman

REGINA SCOTT

Love Inspired

Recycling programs
for this product may
not exist in your area.

™ LOVE INSPIRED BOOKS

ISBN-13: 978-0-373-82893-7

AN HONORABLE GENTLEMAN

Copyright © 2011 by Regina Lundgren

www.LoveInspiredBooks.com

Printed in U.S.A.

For I know the plans I have for you, declares the Lord. Plans to prosper you and not to harm you. Plans to give you hope and a future.
—*Jeremiah* 29:11

To Nonie, who never fails to encourage me; to Linda, who never fails to enlighten; and most of all to my heavenly Father, who never fails to inspire.

Chapter One

Blackcliff Hall, Cumberland, England, 1811

Someone else was in the house.

Sir Trevor Fitzwilliam stopped in the center of the bedchamber he had been considering making his own and listened, head cocked. Blackcliff Hall muttered the usual creaks and groans of a house built nearly two hundred years ago and left for the past two months to itself. He'd already determined the cavernous place to be empty of servants save for an elderly fellow who'd taken his horse at the stables. And servants were generally silent in any regard.

From downstairs came the sound of a door closing. Trevor's head snapped up. He slipped across the Oriental carpet and flattened himself against the heavy oak paneling of the wall. Over the past few years he'd made enemies helping his father and aristocratic friends solve personal problems like blackmail and bribery. Any one of a number of vengeful men could have followed him as he made his way north and east into Cumberland. Any one of them could be searching for him even now.

But if it was a choice of hunt or be hunted, he'd far prefer to hunt.

He glanced out the door, but nothing moved along the wide, oak-paneled corridor that crossed the chamber floor of the gray stone manor house. He knew the main stairs squeaked; he'd frowned at the noise on the way up. From the dust-covered furniture to the cobwebs dulling the brass chandeliers, the place reeked of neglect. The only lamp that was lit was the one he'd set on the bedside table.

How kind of his father to hand the godforsaken place over to him.

Another door closed, and footsteps echoed a moment as the intruder crossed a space of bare wood. From the drawing room to the entry hall, perhaps? He seemed to remember a span of dark wood floor separating the ruby-patterned carpets in the two rooms. If his enemy was anywhere near the entry hall, Trevor would be a fool to take the main stairs down.

Instead, he followed the upstairs corridor for the servants' stair at the end. His footfalls on the thick carpet were silent. The suits of armor that stood sentry in recesses along the corridor watched his passage. He paused only long enough to relieve one of its swords. The blade was long and heavy in his grip, the steel icy. The sword was also dull as ditch water, he had no doubt, but his adversary wouldn't know that. At the very least, it would serve as a club. Trevor slid into the servants' stair and closed the door quietly behind him.

The whitewashed stair was circular, winding up to the schoolroom and down to the main floor, he knew. A window high above let in enough of the fading twilight to allow him to pick his way down. But even as he made the first turn, something moved below. He pulled back before he could be sighted.

There was more than one of them, then.

Hand tight on the sword, breath tight in his chest, he rushed down the final turn, ready to fight for his life. The only thing that moved was the side door, swinging in the cool evening breeze. Outside, a covered walkway swept down to the laundry outbuilding. In the autumn gloom the path stood as empty as the rest of the house had been when he had arrived an hour ago.

He'd known it was chancy at best to show up unannounced for the first time at the estate he'd been given when he'd been made a baronet. He'd expected a flurry of activity to greet his arrival—grooms running to stable his horse, maids hurrying to make up a bed with fresh linens, a chef bustling to prepare him a feast.

But no one had answered his pull of the bell at the gatehouse, and in the end, he had decided to push open the tall wrought-iron gates on his own and ride up the graveled drive. The house was imposing enough, a long block of gray stone, solid and strong, with a separate laundry room a little distance away on one side and kitchen on the other. Trees clustered to the left and right, and gardens lay front and back, but the most visible feature was the black mountain from which the house took its name, rising swiftly in the background.

He had no doubt Blackcliff Hall commanded the west end of the Evendale Valley. Yet, as guardian of the area, it stood unlocked, unlit and unoccupied. Trevor hadn't been expected; he certainly hadn't been welcomed. Now he had to make sure he didn't pay the price for his unheralded arrival with his life.

He shut the side door and shot the bolt, then stood listening a moment. The house was silent around him, as if holding its breath. Where were they?

He eased open the door to the main floor. He knew from his exploration on arrival that the corridor ran past a reception hall on one side and a library and music room on the other to end at the entry hall and the withdrawing room beyond. With the doors closed and the lamps out, the corridor was a black tunnel with a faint gleam of light at the end from the windows flanking the front door. He'd have to pick his way carefully, but right now the shadows were his friends.

Trevor slipped down the corridor, ears straining for a noise to locate his enemy. He hadn't crossed half the space before footsteps thundered up the main stairs. He pulled up short, heart pounding along with the noise.

How many of them were there?

For a moment, he considered leaving. Surely the little village a stone's throw away from the manor boasted a constable. If Trevor could get to the stables, no horse could catch Icarus. He glanced back at the door to the servants' stair and the outdoors.

All your life you've wanted something of your own. Will you let them steal this from you, as well?

He wasn't sure where the thoughts came from; he didn't think to ask. He knew in his heart they were right. He squared his shoulders and faced front again. Derelict or not, this was his home now. He had plans for it. He would leave only when he was ready.

He crept down the corridor for the entryway, debating his choices. He could follow them up the stairs, but they'd hear him coming. He could wait at the bottom, but they'd have momentum on their side. He needed something to stop them, to trip them up so he could gain the upper hand.

He reached the entry hall and darted across, careful to keep his boot heels from touching the parquet floor. The furniture in all the rooms was of massive mahogany. Moving it would take time he didn't have, and even in the dim light he thought they'd see it on the stair.

But, if he remembered correctly, a stone statue

of a shepherd, about knee high, rested in the corner. Placed partway up the stairs, the cheery lad would make an excellent stumbling block. Trevor slid into the corner and frowned. The space was empty, and he thought he could make out a bare spot in the dust of the floor. The shepherd, it seemed, had seen fit to move since Trevor had passed him an hour ago.

What would anyone want with a stone shepherd?

Nearby, wood scraped on wood. At least one of them was on the main floor then, but doing what, Trevor couldn't know. Why didn't they come for him? Had he mistaken their purpose? Was it Trevor they wanted or the house's treasures? Either way, he wasn't going to give up without a fight.

He backed into the withdrawing room and looked around. Someone had left a lantern, partially hooded, near the bow window. The glow bathed the settee, sturdy armchairs, wood-wrapped hearth and sundry side tables in gold, and left the back of the room draped in shadow. He hadn't done more than glance in here when he'd arrived, but he didn't think anything was missing.

Indeed, something had been added. The stone shepherd was standing in the center of the bloodred pattern of the carpet.

A chill ran up Trevor. But he didn't believe in ghosts, or statues that moved by themselves. Some days he wasn't even sure he believed in God, at least not a god who cared for humankind. His life was proof that a gentleman only had himself to rely on.

But what would his enemies want with a statue, and why had they abandoned it? Keeping an eye out for movement, he crossed to the statue and picked it up with his free hand.

The piece was heavier than he expected, the stone cold in his grip. He jiggled it up and down, but nothing rattled to indicate a secret compartment. He turned it front to back, but in the dim light he couldn't even be sure of the stone used to carve it, let alone any distinguishing marks.

"Put that down."

Fool! Why had he looked down, even for an instant? Trevor turned slowly toward the voice, ready for anything. What he'd taken as a solid wall across the back of the withdrawing room was clearly a pocket door allowing access to the dining room beyond. Framed in the doorway was a cloaked figure, shorter and slighter than him, a lad by the timbre of his voice. Trevor could have taken him easily, if it weren't for the pistol extending from the shadows in his gloved hand.

"Is it valuable, then?" Trevor asked, making a show of eyeing the statue even as he eased closer across the carpet toward the fellow.

"You wouldn't have come to steal it if you didn't think so," the lad countered.

Trevor cocked a smile and took another step closer. "Takes one to know one, eh? What are you after?"

The pistol was lifted to aim at his heart. "Anyone

who dares disturb this house. Now— Put. That. Down."

"Certainly," Trevor said. "Catch." He hurled the statue at the fellow and dove into its wake. The statue fell with a thud against the carpet, and Trevor and the intruder went down in a tangle of arms and legs, sword snared in the cloak.

The pistol roared, the flash blinding him for a moment. His heart jerked, but he felt no wrenching pain, no blow from a lead ball.

"Now look what you've done!" his captive cried, obviously unhurt, as well. "Dolly! Dolly, here!"

In that second, Trevor realized two things. Something very large was thundering back down the stairs.

And the person he held pinned to the floor was a woman.

Gwendolyn Allbridge glared up at the man who held her flattened to the carpet. With the lantern across the room and behind him, all she could make out was height and strength. The arms that pushed on her shoulders were like pillars of polished oak. She wiggled against the pressure but only managed to press herself deeper into the pile of the carpet.

"Let me up!" she demanded. "Dolly!"

To her surprise, he immediately released her and rose. She scrambled to her feet, breath coming in gasps. Taking a step back, she nearly tripped over the useless pistol, its single ball spent. She should have brought both her father's pistols. She should have woken her father and made him come up to the house to investigate the strange lights himself. She was unarmed and alone with a looter in an empty house, and no one would hear her if she screamed.

Well, no human, perhaps. Dolly bounded through the door, a dappled mountain that only looked larger with the shadows thrown by the lantern. The mastiff took one look at the intruder and bared her teeth. Her growl reverberated through the room.

"What on earth?" he said. "You have a trained bear?"

She smiled at his confusion. Dolly was the largest mastiff ever bred in the Evendale Valley. Her massive head reached above Gwen's waist, and, at nearly two hundred pounds, she outweighed her mistress by over sixty.

"She doesn't like strangers," Gwen said. "I'd leave now if I were you."

Dolly let out a bark, deep and demanding, and he took a step back.

"I fear I have two problems with leaving," he said, and she was a little disappointed he didn't sound more terrified. In fact, he didn't sound like the vagrant she'd expected. His voice was educated, cultivated. And, if she didn't know better, she'd have thought he was amused.

"And what would those be?" she asked sweetly while Dolly growled and prowled closer to him.

"Your bear is standing between me and the door,"

he replied. Then he turned his head to look at her. "And I own this house."

The owner?

Gwen's breath left her lungs in a rush. But it couldn't be. They'd received no word, seen no one at the gate. Two months had gone by since Colonel Umbrey, the previous owner, had passed on, and they'd only just heard the estate had been sold.

"Prove it," she challenged.

He sketched her a bow that made Dolly pull up with a grunt of surprise.

"Sir Trevor Fitzwilliam, baronet, of Blackcliff Hall," he said, "at your service. And you would be?"

"Unconvinced," Gwen said. "Dolly, come!"

The mastiff edged around him and pressed herself against Gwen's side. Now that her pulse was calming, Gwen felt every bruise along her backside. She'd have to use some of her mother's liniment tonight. Leaning into the dog's strength, Gwen crossed to the table in front of the bow window, where she'd set and hooded her lantern on arrival to avoid detection. As she opened the hood, she turned and let light flood the space.

Oh, but he was a handsome one! Raven-haired, square-jawed, with features clean and firm. She couldn't be sure of the color of his eyes—blue like her father's? Brown like hers? Green?—but they were deep set and narrowed now as he considered her.

What did he see? A slip of a woman with untamable auburn curls and a pert nose? She was certain she didn't look like the respectable daughter of the estate's former steward. The brown cloak was slipping off the shoulders of her green wool gown, and both were wrinkled from her collision with the floor.

On the other hand, she could well believe he was the master of the house. His navy coat was cut to emphasize the breadth of his shoulders, and his fawn trousers hugged muscular thighs. The lantern light glinted off the gold filigree buttons on his satin-striped waistcoat, and a gemstone winked from the hopelessly rumpled folds of his snowy cravat.

Oh, Lord, what have I done!

"If you could provide proof of your identity, sir," she said, knowing her voice sounded decidedly fainter, "I would be pleased to welcome you properly to Blackcliff Hall."

Sir Trevor's mouth curved up in a smile that was perilously close to a smirk. "My papers are upstairs. Do you trust me to fetch them, or would you and your bear like to accompany me?"

She probably should, just in case he was lying and had friends or a pistol waiting. After all, she had seen a light moving in the house earlier. That's why she'd come up to investigate with Dolly.

The house had been broken into three times in the past two months. Her father would find a door left swinging or a window wide open on his rounds about the estate. She'd helped him inventory the rooms each time, but they'd never been able to determine that anything had been taken or even disturbed.

Vagrants, Mr. Casperson the constable was sure, although the look he directed toward her father was knowing. He suspected Horace Allbridge of neglecting his duty, either by failing to protect the property he currently served as caretaker or by siphoning off its treasures, selling them himself and blaming mysterious others.

Gwen bristled just thinking about the unfair accusation. *Help me, Lord. Help me show them how wrong they are.*

"I'd be delighted to wait here," she said.

He snapped her a bow and strode from the room. Gwen followed him to the door and watched as he started up the stairs, which squeaked at the fall of his high black boots.

It seemed the master of Blackcliff had arrived at last. But would he be the man Gwen had prayed for?

Chapter Two

The moment Sir Trevor turned the corner for the upper floor, Gwen burst into action. She tugged the carpet back into place where their struggle had creased it, then pulled off her cloak and used it to wipe the dust from the side tables and mantel. She shook out the dust in the dining room (time later to clean *that*) and left the cloak out of sight on the embroidered seat of one of the mahogany chairs.

Returning to the withdrawing room, she picked up the sword he'd left lying on the carpet and was surprised to find that it looked familiar. Had he taken it from the ancient armor upstairs? Wrinkling her nose, she tucked it into a corner to return later.

But the sword wasn't the only thing that needed returning. She located the shepherd statue rolled against the wall and went to right it. The soft white marble glowed with life; she could feel the shepherd's vigilance in guarding his sheep, his eyes narrowed into the distance, one hand against his brow, the other gripping his staff.

I am the good shepherd, and know my sheep and am known of mine.

She smiled at the familiar verse, but her smile quickly faded into a frown. Why had Sir Trevor moved it to the center of the withdrawing room, where she'd seen it when she'd arrived earlier? He could hardly be redecorating so soon. And if he was, he wasn't very practical. Why would he want to trip over a statue every time he crossed the room?

She picked it up and nearly tripped herself. Sir Trevor must be as strong as he looked, for she had trouble carrying it back to the entry hall. Dolly padded alongside her, pink tongue lolling out crookedly from her heavy jowls, her breath coming in huffs of delight to be up and moving.

"We must make a better impression on him," Gwen told her as she returned to the withdrawing room. She snatched the tinderbox from the mantel and set about lighting the brass lamps that rested here and there among the tables. The light gleamed off the heavy oak paneling that ran through the house and veined the ceilings and stairwells. Blackcliff Hall could be warm and welcoming, solid and safe. She had to show him that.

"This is what Father needs," she said to Dolly, "to serve a respectable master in a respectable position. That ought to get his mind off his troubles."

Of course, it wouldn't hurt if she looked a bit

more respectable herself, she realized. She paused to pin back her wayward curls into the bun at the top of her head, straighten her white lace collar and smooth the wrinkles in her green wool gown.

Goodness, were her fingers trembling? She mustn't show how much Sir Trevor's arrival meant to her and her father. From this moment forward, she vowed, the new master of Blackcliff would be met with nothing but pleasantries. She was standing by the hearth with a smile on her face, Dolly lying calmly at her feet, when Sir Trevor strode back in a moment later.

He pulled up short and gaped at her. She knew admiration when she saw it, and she couldn't help the satisfaction that shot through her.

"Pardon me, madam," he said, quirking a smile, "but there was a miscreant here with a pet bear a few moments ago. Do you know where they went?"

"La, but I'm sure they're miles away," Gwen answered, grin forming at his teasing tone. Then she dipped a curtsy. "Miss Gwendolyn Allbridge, sir. My father and I reside in your gatehouse. And this is Dolly."

The mastiff's tail thumped twice, and Dolly raised her dark head to gaze at him, jowls widening in a grin.

He bowed. "A pleasure to meet you, Miss Dolly, Miss Allbridge. May I ask how you came to be in my house this fine evening?"

His voice was more curious than accusing. "My

father has been acting as caretaker while the house went through Probate and was sold," she explained. "Dolly and I spied your light when we were walking and came to investigate."

He raised a brow. "Your father must be infirm, then."

Gwen stiffened. "Not at all! Who told you that?"

"No one." He crossed to her side and stood towering over her. Her head fit under his arm. She ought to feel menaced, but, with him smiling down at her, she felt as protected as when Dolly pressed close to her side.

"I stopped at the gatehouse when I arrived this evening," he said. "No one answered the bell. And your father saw fit to send you when there was a stranger in the house. Naturally I assumed he must be ill."

"My father was...unavailable earlier," Gwen replied, hoping he wouldn't ask the reason. It had only been a few cups tonight, far less than the bottles he'd downed shortly after Mother had died. "I was out with Dolly checking the grounds for the night, or I would have answered the bell myself."

He frowned. "You serve as night watchman, as well?"

Night watchman, nurse, gardener and cook, but she could hardly tell him all that without making her father sound like a laggard. "Only when my father is unavailable, I assure you."

He glanced around the room. "And who serves as maid?"

Not her, and for that he should be thankful. With the lamps lit, she could see streaks of dust crossing the fine grain of the wood where she'd missed spots in her hurry. "The staff were all let go when Colonel Umbrey, the previous owner, died. His heir chose to sell the estate, and we couldn't know when someone would purchase it."

His gaze speared her. His eyes were green, a light shade like the creamy jade Colonel Umbrey had brought back from his travels in India and the Orient. "And you've never heard of Holland covers?"

"Certainly we've heard of covering the furniture when it's unused," Gwen said, trying not to sound defensive. *Pleasantries, remember?* It wouldn't do to snap at her father's new employer.

But he couldn't know how hard she had to work to get anything done around here, the hours spent cajoling and encouraging for the least task. Ever since her mother had died a year ago, her father had lost all will to live. And losing the respect of the villagers hadn't helped. Far too many things had changed at Blackcliff. What they needed was a little order.

"We were waiting to hear from the new master before giving the place a good cleaning," she explained at his frown. "The solicitor only just reported that Blackcliff had been sold. We certainly didn't expect you to arrive unannounced."

"A gentleman shouldn't need to announce his arrival when returning home," he said, not unkindly, and handed her a leather-bound packet.

"Well, it is a new home for you," Gwen pointed out, untying the ribbon that held the packet shut. "And we thought if you were going to make Blackcliff your home, you would arrive with more ceremony. Do you have a carriage somewhere? Luggage?"

"I rode," he said, and nothing in his tone gave her any clue as to why or how long he intended to stay.

Did he live in the Evendale Valley, then, and it had been merely a short ride to reach the house? No, that voice belonged in a more sophisticated setting. Or was this only one of the many properties he must inspect over the course of a year?

Gwen glanced down at the parchment, hoping for a few answers to the questions she could not ask without seeming even more impertinent. She'd seen enough legal papers as she'd helped her father act as steward for the colonel to be able to locate the important details in the close-written document. She glanced up at him, blinking.

"You were awarded the estate for services to the Crown? Were you a soldier like Colonel Umbrey?"

He smiled, but the light didn't reach his cool green eyes. "Nothing so dashing. I settled a thorny administrative matter, and the chief beneficiary saw fit to recommend me to the Prince and purchase an estate in thanks. I take it you're satisfied that I'm the new owner."

She could not see him sitting behind a desk, shuffling papers, fingers smeared with ink. Those large hands looked like they should be wielding a sword as they had been earlier or clutching the reins of a team of horses. Despite his title of baronet, Sir Trevor seemed far too healthy, too vital, to have spent his life either clerking or in idle pursuit of pleasure.

But the papers looked as legal as any she'd seen. She slipped them back into the leather covering.

"This all appears to be in order," she replied, handing the packet to him. She squared her shoulders and gave him her most charming smile. "Welcome to Blackcliff Hall, Sir Trevor. I hope you will consider it your home and wish to spend your life here. Now let's get you down to the George and see you settled."

In the act of accepting the packet from her, Trevor paused. A singular woman. Energy glowed from her fiery hair to her creamy skin to the fluttering of her gloved hands. Her topics moved as rapidly as she did. "The George?" he asked.

"The George Inn. Fine establishment. Excellent cook. You'll love it." She slapped her thigh, and Dolly scrambled to her feet, nails clattering against the stone of the hearth.

Now that the lamps had been properly lit he could see the mastiff more clearly. Her body, dappled in streaks of dun and black, was thick and powerful, with a barrel chest and a solid column of a neck. Her muzzle was coal-black, and her jowls quivered in her eagerness to move. Intelligence sat in those big brown eyes, and he was certain loyalty filled her massive heart. He could only be thankful she was so well trained, for even his dull club of a sword would have been of little use against her had she chosen to attack him.

"There's no need to go to an inn," he said to Gwen, but she was already bustling about the room, retrieving her lantern, extinguishing the other lamps. Everything about her said determination, from the set of her pointed chin to the quick movements of her lithe body. She looked to be a few years younger than his thirty years, and he wondered why such a beautiful woman wasn't married and instead prowling around his estate in the dark with only a great beast of a dog for company.

"There's every need," she assured him, retrieving her cloak and throwing it around her shoulders. He hadn't noticed the streaks mottling the soft brown wool of the garment. Had he caused that when he'd knocked her down?

"You may not have had time to visit every room in the house," she said, returning to his side, "but few are livable. The beds need airing, the lamps trimming and the pantry stocking." She smiled at him. "I'll have everything ready by the time you return tomorrow."

From anyone else, the statement would have been laughable. He *had* looked in every room in the house earlier, and he knew how much work had to be done to make it a home. But, with the light shining in her deep brown eyes, her face turned up to his, he thought this woman could very well work miracles.

"I'd prefer to stay here," he said, and even he could hear how stubborn he sounded.

Her smile turned kind. "Now, now," she said, laying her free hand on his arm with a grip that was firmer than he would have guessed from the size of her, "we must make sure you have a pleasant evening. I'm certain you'd prefer a good bed tonight and a nice warm dinner. You cannot possibly get that here. Why should you settle for less than the best? Where's your horse?"

She was tugging him toward the entryway, and Trevor followed, feeling as if he'd been snatched up in the middle of a storm. "He's in the stable."

She tsked. "I'm surprised we had feed for him. I'll see to that, as well. Or rather, my father will. He's very good at making sure all the master's needs are met." She cast him a glance out of the corners of her eyes. "He was the steward before Colonel Umbrey died. Did they tell you that when they awarded you the place?"

"No," Trevor said as she released him to hustle

to the front door, the dog trotting obediently at her side. "I assumed the estate came adequately staffed. But I'm used to roughing it. I assure you I'll be fine here tonight."

"Nonsense. We can't have the new master living in anything less than comfort." She paused to smile back at him, and the look tugged at his heart as surely as her hand had tugged at his arm. Was this how Greek sailors felt in the myth of the siren? Her beauty and enthusiasm called to him, but he had a feeling they'd lead him far from his intended course.

"You're not going to give me a moment's peace until I've agreed to this, are you?" he asked, certain he knew the answer.

Her dark eyes crinkled up as if she was laughing inside. "Why, Sir Trevor, I simply want to make sure you are well taken care of. My father would insist on nothing less."

He was beginning to think her father was at home, hiding from her determination. If anyone insisted on anything in that house, he was certain he was looking at her.

"And will your father be here to greet me in the morning?" he countered.

Her smile widened. "I guarantee it. I'm certain once you see the estate in the morning light, you'll be pleased to call it yours. Would you prefer to ride to the village or shall we walk? It isn't far."

He didn't like losing, even an argument, but he

had to agree with her that the house needed work before it would be comfortable.

He wasn't sure why that so disappointed him. He'd decided on the way north that he would only use the place for the income it could provide. He'd never intended to make it home. Home was London, the social whirl, the acquaintances he'd made in school and afterward. The sooner he could settle his affairs in Blackcliff Hall, the sooner he could return.

"I'll ride," he said, striding for the door. "That is, if the groom can be bothered to saddle my horse."

"I'm afraid the groom gave notice ages ago," she said in that calm, conciliatory voice. She followed him out the door, the mastiff bounding down the stone steps ahead of them while she turned to lock the door. "Colonel Umbrey decided he was too old to move from the Hall and sold his carriage and horses."

Was that what would become of him if he stayed? Would he grow to be a fat, complacent old man with no interest in even making the short ride into town?

"Then the fellow who's staying in the stables," Trevor all but snapped.

She handed him the ornate brass key, which weighed more heavily than it should in his hand. "No one lives at the estate except me and my father, Sir Trevor."

He stared at her, feeling as if her great bear of a dog had sat on his chest. "Then who on earth took charge of my horse?"

Chapter Three

Lord, please protect his horse!

Gwen threw up the prayer as she led Sir Trevor around the side of the house and through a door in the stone wall for the stables. She could tell the animal meant a great deal to him. In the light of her lantern, his face was tight, his jaw hard. His long legs ate up the ground as they crossed the garden at the back of the house. She had to scurry to keep up.

Dolly obviously thought it was as great game, this rush through the growing dark, the garden silent around them. She bounded alongside Sir Trevor, veering off from time to time into the shadows to snuff at something under the weed-choked plants. Sir Trevor, on the other hand, had his eyes narrowed in such a fierce look that Gwen could only pray the person who'd taken charge of his horse was either a highly competent stranger looking for work, or was miles away by now.

"We've had a little trouble with vagrants," she offered as they approached the long, two-story building of dark stone at the back of the garden. "Nothing's been stolen, mind you. I'm sure it's just men out of work, on their way to the next village and needing a place to stay the night."

"And a horse to ride," he said, voice as tight as his look.

Lord, not his horse! She needed Sir Trevor to love the place; she needed him to want to stay. It was the only way to save the village.

She hadn't done more than check the stables for vagrants in the past two months, so she wasn't surprised to find it dark as they approached. Her lantern's light glinted off the half-moon windows that topped the arches in the stone. More weeds poked up among the gravel of the yard.

The big wooden door blocking the entrance protested as she tried to pull it open. With a grimace of impatience, he took the tarnished brass handle from her grip and tugged. The door moved out of the way with an unearthly screech that made Dolly yelp in protest.

"A little oil will fix that right up," she assured him as he pushed past her into the stables. The scent of decaying hay and dried manure tickled her nose, and she sneezed. Oh, what must he think of them!

Even as Gwen raised her lantern, Dolly trotted down the wide breezeway between the rows of stalls. It had been an elegant stable once, the boxes lacquered black and the curving screen separating the tops of the stalls a pristine white. Now everything looked a dingy gray. When had she allowed things to get away from her?

Something whinnied in the darkness beyond the light. Sir Trevor let out a breath of obvious relief and stalked toward the sound. Gwen followed him, then pulled up with a gasp.

In truth, she'd wondered why he had been quite so worked up about a horse. She knew they could cost a pretty penny, but, in her experience, they were great hawking beasts like as not to step on your foot as to pull your coach.

The animal standing in the middle stall, however, wasn't a horse any more than a diamond was a rock. This animal had a jet-black coat that gleamed like satin and warm, liquid brown eyes that demanded loyalty. Every line of muscle and tendon said power.

"Dolly, no!" Gwen ordered as the mastiff approached the rope that closed off the stall. But the magnificent horse merely lowered its head and blew a breath at the dog. Dolly's tail wagged so happily her whole rump wiggled.

Sir Trevor strode up to his horse and stroked the long muzzle. "Good lad, easy now. Everything all right here?"

She wouldn't have been surprised if the horse had answered him. The beast tossed his head with a jingle, and she realized he still wore his bridle.

"Never even removed the saddle," Sir Trevor

said, and his tone indicated he felt the lapse worthy of eternal punishment. "Still, I suppose I should just be thankful he didn't make off with you."

"I'm very sorry," Gwen felt compelled to say. "I can't imagine who met you out here."

"Neither can I," he replied, gently nudging Dolly aside with his knee so he could release the rope. "But I assure you I had better not see him again."

Please, Lord, let it be someone besides Father!

"Certainly not," she agreed, moving forward to latch her free hand on Dolly's collar and pull the mastiff out of the way. The dog came reluctantly, clearly wanting to sniff about this fascinating creature they'd found in the stables. "Is your horse all right?"

He'd stepped into the stall and was running his hands over the animal as if to make sure, his movements gentle, soothing. Why had she thought he was meant for battle? She could imagine those hands playing a sonata or painting a masterpiece just as passionately.

"He seems to be unharmed," he murmured, and she could feel his relief.

Gwen ventured closer, peering through the spindles of the upper screen on the box. The golden light from her lantern warmed horse and master alike, glowing in their dark hair. "What's his name?"

"Icarus." The word brought a smile to his lips, and Gwen felt her lips turning up in response. He patted the horse on its glossy flank. "He likes to fly higher than he should."

She wondered if the same could be said of his master. "He's beautiful."

"That he is. A descendant from the Byerley Turk." He dropped his hand and turned. His face was solemn, troubled, and she stood a little taller to hear his concerns.

"Tell me the truth, Miss Allbridge. Can this estate provide anyone a living?"

She hoped so; she prayed so. Everything she'd ever dreamed of depended on it. "Certainly!" she told him, putting every ounce of faith into the word. "It was the finest estate in the upper valley before the colonel took ill. All it needs is a little attention."

Trevor glanced around the stable. Stalls just like the one in which he stood stretched away on either side. The place would hold a dozen horses and several carriages when full, with room for coachman and grooms in the quarters upstairs. Now the darkness surrounded them like smoke, and she thought she could hear the scurrying of tiny feet not far away.

"I suspect," he said with a sigh, "that it also needs an influx of cash."

She dimpled at him. "Well, that goes without saying."

He closed his eyes a moment. Was he praying? Did it truly look so awful to him that he had to reach to God for help? She wanted to touch him, stroke away the worried lines from his eyes and mouth. But that was not her place. All she could offer was encouragement.

"It will look brighter in the morning," she murmured. "I promise."

He opened his eyes and regarded her. Perhaps it was a trick of the lantern light, but his jade eyes seemed to have warmed. She felt warm just gazing into them. The vast stable was suddenly too small, too intimate. She swallowed and turned for the door. "I'll just show you to the George now, shall I?"

She took a deep breath to steady herself and glanced back in time to see him swing himself easily into the saddle. "If it's in your village, I'll find it. Have your father send down my shaving kit. And tell him I expect a full report tomorrow morning in the library at ten."

With a cluck of encouragement, the magnificent Sir Trevor and his equally magnificent horse disappeared into the night.

An influx of cash. Trevor shook his head as Icarus picked his way down the graveled drive. Gwen Allbridge smiled as if finding money was an easy matter. He supposed it would be for many a gentleman. But she couldn't know that he was a gentleman in title only.

It had ever been this way. He had been born outside of wedlock, to a mother who was considered no lady. Yet his mother, his father, the accountants who arranged for him to attend the best schools, to wear the finest clothes, expected him to act the gentleman. Nay, they demanded it of him.

Gentlemen did not sully their hands with work; gentlemen lived off the income from their estates or their shrewd investments in the 'Change. But when you were born to neither estate nor investment, when the money was provided merely to educate, clothe and feed you while you were a lad, how were you supposed to get on?

He'd found a way, but few respected it. If the determined Miss Allbridge knew how he'd earned his meager income and his baronetcy, he had little doubt she would be far less eager to welcome him to her village.

But she wasn't the only one so eager, he quickly learned. He located the George easily enough: a two-story, whitewashed building with black shutters and the picture of the king swinging merrily from the sign over the red front door. The inn was located in the heart of the little village, surrounded by tile-roofed cottages and two glass-fronted shops, all dark for the night.

The tall, long-nosed innkeeper was all politeness as he made sure Icarus was rubbed down and stabled. He easily agreed to have Trevor take a room for the night on the upper floor. That is, until he read Trevor's entry in the great register book lying open on a high table near the entry.

"Sir Trevor Fitzwilliam of Blackcliff?" He

squinted down at the words in black ink on the wide-lined book, then jerked up his head on his long neck like a stork checking for foxes. "Mrs. Billings—do you hear that? We are housing the new master of Blackcliff!"

Only three men lounged in the public room behind Trevor, but he could hear them muttering, the scrape of a chair as someone rose as if to get a better look at him. The pudgy innkeeper's wife waddled from the steaming kitchen, wiping her hands on her wrinkled apron. Her brown eyes were bright as sugared raisins. "The master himself? Oh, an honor, sir, to be sure!"

In short order, he'd been installed in what he was assured was the best room in the house, jacket taken to be cleaned and pressed, pan warming the huge bed while a dinner of spiced mutton, soft pudding and buttered squash warmed his insides. Now that was more like it, that was what he'd hoped to find at Blackcliff—diffidence, competence, respect.

The morning was even better, with a breakfast of eggs and country ham, sharp cheddar, grilled tomatoes fresh from the vine and applesauce loaded with cinnamon, all with a week-old London *Times* to keep him company.

And there was the announcement: "Trevor Fitzwilliam, elevated to the rank of baronet. It appears that nepotism is still alive and well in our fair empire." He crushed the paper with his fist.

So he wasn't the only one to see his father's hand

in all this. Could the duke have found a more out-of-the-way place to send the son he refused to acknowledge publicly? There wasn't an estate in Devon or Lincolnshire he could have purchased? No, Trevor must be sent about as far north as possible, into the Evendale Valley to the west of Carlisle, well into the peaks and lakes of Cumberland.

But, as always, Trevor had acted as a gentleman. He'd come to look at his estate, assess its ability to provide him an income. He would see that all assets of his land were producing, make sure his tenants were cared for and capable.

But nothing said he had to stay.

He had asked that Icarus be ready for him by half past nine, but he hadn't expected the crowd waiting for him when he exited the George. Nearly two dozen men, women and children crowded expectantly in the coaching yard behind the inn. They wore rough cottons and dark wools, patched and frayed but generally clean. Their faces were pinched, their eyes wide. He couldn't think what they wanted from him, but the moment he stepped out, a cheer went up.

Trevor raised his brows.

Then Gwen Allbridge shouldered her way to the front. Today she looked every inch the lady, her coppery curls barely visible inside a white satin-lined straw bonnet, her slender body wrapped in a dark green coat with a ruffled collar and lace at the cuffs, tied under her bosom with a rose-colored ribbon. He felt himself smiling at the sight of her and knew it wasn't just because she was the most friendly face in the crowd.

"Good morning, Sir Trevor," she said with a bob of a curtsy that set her pink bow to fluttering. "I hope you don't mind, but a few of the villagers asked permission to accompany you to the Hall this morning."

Trevor felt like standing a little taller. He offered them all a polite smile, in keeping with his new role of lord of the manor. "I am the one honored, I assure you."

An approving murmur ran through the crowd. Gwen stepped aside, and an aisle opened between him and Icarus, who stood, head high, as if deigning to receive the attention bestowed upon him.

Trevor rather felt the same. He strolled down the center, nodding to this person and that, all the while keeping an eye out for the man who'd taken Icarus from him the night before or any of the men he had crossed in London. No one looked the least familiar. In fact, they were thin-faced and weary, as if living this close to the fells sapped their strength.

An older woman in a faded skirt curtsied to him. "Welcome to Blackcliff, sir. If you've need of a maid, my Becky's a hard worker." The plain-faced young woman next to her stared at him with worshipful eyes.

Gwen laid a hand on the woman's arm as if in encouragement. "Sir Trevor will be making decisions on staffing soon, I promise. Send Becky up to me tomorrow, Mrs. Dennison, and I'll find work for her."

The woman's blue eyes filled with tears. "Oh, thank you, Miss Allbridge."

Trevor suddenly felt as if fine threads were being woven around him, tying him to this place. He wanted to shake them off, demand his independence. He had come north to learn what Blackcliff Hall could do for him, not what he could do for it.

Mrs. Dennison licked her lips. "And while you're making plans for the place, sir, I hope you'll see fit to reopen the mine."

Silence fell, stretched. They were all watching him. He wouldn't have been surprised had they been holding their breaths. But this was one question he felt perfectly comfortable answering.

He smiled at the woman. "If there's a producing mine on my land, you can be sure I'll have it opened."

Another cheer went up. Hats were launched into the air. Couples embraced. Mrs. Dennison was openly crying now.

Gwen Allbridge grabbed his arm and yanked him toward Icarus.

"Now you've done it," she said, dark eyes narrowed. "If I were you, I'd ride hard for the Hall and not look back."

Chapter Four

Of course, Sir Trevor ignored her advice. In fact, Gwen was beginning to think the baronet was not going to be an easy gentleman to manage.

He kept his head high as his horse stepped away from the inn, the crowd cavorting along behind him as he made his stately way up the winding, tree-shaded lane. He must know the hope he'd given them—their faces glowed and their praises rang to the fells. Walking beside him, she could look up at his face—calm, dignified, with the barest hint of a smile lingering about the curve of his lips. He obviously had no idea that what he'd promised was impossible.

Oh, Lord, please keep them from hating him when he has to tell them the truth!

At least he wasn't gloating, she thought as they approached the wrought-iron gates of Blackcliff Hall. However much of a challenge he offered her in keeping the estate going, he had to be a better owner than Colonel Umbrey. The colonel had always been capricious—the house too warm one day, too cold the next; salmon his favorite and least favorite meal by turns. He'd only grown more strange as the years had passed. Look at how he'd cast off his faithful valet, discharged her father and holed up in his bed-chamber.

But even he had understood that the mine was closed.

The villagers stopped respectfully outside the gates, their rousing cheers following Gwen and Trevor up the curving gravel drive. The trees edging the estate boundary quickly hid them from view. From the direction of the gatehouse came a single, questioning bark: Dolly, protesting being left behind. She hated it when Gwen locked her in the kennel behind the stone gatehouse. Gwen would have liked nothing better than to lean against Dolly's warm side, particularly as Gwen was a bit sore from the night's exertions.

But she knew the mastiff had no place in the morning's activities. This morning was all for Sir Trevor.

As they continued up the drive, other noises faded until the loudest sound was the crunch of Icarus's hooves against rough gravel. The autumn breeze brushed Gwen's cheek, set the trees along the drive to rustling. Leaves of bright red and deep russet drifted down across the emerald lawn.

"How long has Blackcliff been sitting?" Sir Trevor asked.

Did it look so terrible to him, even in the daylight? True, the stone fountain below the sweep of the drive stood empty and clogged with fallen leaves, but that was easily fixed. "About six months," Gwen replied. "Colonel Umbrey refused all callers the last three months of his life, and he wouldn't allow any changes to the estate. But the mine's been closed for over a year. The surveyors said it was too dangerous to work."

There—she'd said it. She cast him a quick glance to see how he might be taking it. The smile on his handsome face was even more noticeable.

"Surveyors can be mistaken," he said.

So could he, but Gwen was suddenly very glad his education was one thing she could leave to her father.

Rob Winslow was waiting in front of the gray stone manor to take Icarus. She'd picked Rob purposely. He was tall, his strapping frame showed well in the brown coat and breeches that had been the livery of the previous master, he knew something about horses being the son of the village blacksmith and he'd play the role for no other pay than her thanks. He touched his brown forelock as Sir Trevor reined in, then quickly took charge of the horse.

Sir Trevor watched him, green eyes narrowed,

until he'd disappeared around the house for the stables.

Gwen swallowed, feeling the chill in the air. "He's not the one who took your horse yesterday, is he?"

"No. That man was much older and considerably thinner. That was my impression, at least. He was wearing a cloak." Sir Trevor shook himself and started up the stairs. "I thought you said the groom had been discharged."

"He was," Gwen said, pacing him to the door. "Rob, that is Mr. Winslow, is merely filling in until you settle on your staff."

He raised his dark brows over his aristocratic nose. He'd taken out his key, but she reached around him for the door. "No need. My father's already opened the house. You did ask to meet with him this morning."

He cast her a look. She could not tell what he was thinking, but she found herself holding her breath as he pushed open the door and strode inside.

Margaret Bentley was waiting to take his coat. She was the one person Gwen had qualms about. Oh, she looked the part of housekeeper with her snowy hair bound in a coronet about her round face and her motherly girth swathed in black bombazine covered by a pristine white apron. But she had no experience as a cook for anyone other than her six children and husband, all of whom had passed on.

"Welcome home, sir," she said in her gentle voice

as she reached up to help Sir Trevor with his multi-caped greatcoat. She had to stand on her tiptoes to pull it off. As she dropped back down, she peered at Gwen around his waist, brows up and mouth pursed in an O of awe.

"This is Mrs. Bentley," Gwen said. The little woman straightened as Sir Trevor turned to eye her. "She's acting as housekeeper and cook."

Mrs. Bentley bobbed a curtsy, puddling Sir Trevor's coat against the floor as she did so. "A pleasure, sir. Mr. Allbridge is waiting in the library, and I've started the teakettle on the boil. Is there anything else I can do for you?"

"No, thank you," Trevor replied. "And tea would be most welcome."

Gwen let out her breath.

"Have it right out, dearie," Mrs. Bentley said with a grin, then she blinked and swallowed. "That is, very good, sir." She ducked her head and hurried off.

Trevor turned to Gwen. "So I have a groom and a housekeeper. How many more?"

"A maid of all work, and I'm working on a footman," Gwen replied, feeling rather proud of herself. It hadn't been easy finding people willing to volunteer with such short notice. "And several other men will be by this afternoon to set the gardens to rights."

She waited for his praise, his amazement over her

skills at managing a house. She was certain she'd be just as humble accepting them.

Instead, his mouth tightened. "You are kind to think of my needs, but in the future, I'd prefer to be consulted before you spend my money."

Gwen felt as if he'd slapped her. She recoiled, but only for a moment. How dare he assume she'd spend his money without asking!

She squared her shoulders and looked up into his icy green gaze. "I will have you know, sir, that not one of these people asked a penny. Blackcliff Hall is the life of this village, and we're all so glad to see it occupied again that we were delighted to stay up last night and make it presentable. And if you were any kind of gentleman, you'd appreciate that!"

Trevor raised his brows at her vehemence. Every inch of her straightened spine and high head said righteous indignation. Her chest rose and fell in her green coat, pink ribbon fluttering, as if she were taking deep breaths to try to steady her emotions. She truly thought these people would serve him with no expectation of reward.

He couldn't believe that. In his experience, everyone had a reason for offering help; everyone expected something in return. Nor could he believe they'd worked all night for no other purpose than to pretty up Blackcliff Hall. They knew nothing about him. Why put themselves out on his behalf?

And despite what she'd said about Blackcliff

being vital to the village, he was certain they must have more important things to do. Determined to prove himself right, he strode into the withdrawing room.

And stopped. And stared.

Every wood surface glowed; every inch of brass from the candlesticks on the mantel to the lamps on the tables gleamed. A fire was crackling in the hearth, and a bunch of russet chrysanthemums filled a crystal vase on one of the decorative tables. He could smell the lemon polish.

He whirled to find Gwen watching him. "Is the whole house like this?" he demanded.

A becoming shade of pink darkened her cheeks. "Most of it. We didn't quite get to the cellar, but we hoped you wouldn't get to it, either."

He glanced around the room again, noting the quilted lap robe draping the sofa and the silhouette framed on the wall. Neither had been there last night, he was certain. "Did you sleep at all?" he marveled.

She smiled. "Who could sleep with a new master at Blackcliff?"

Trevor shook his head. It seemed he was wrong. They truly had stayed up all night, for him. What kind of people were these? What land had his father sent him to? There had to be some reason for their kindness, but if not expectation of repayment, then what?

Still, he knew what his response must be. He offered her a deep bow. "You have my thanks, Miss Allbridge, and my apology. I'm not used to people so generous with their time and talents."

"You've never met the people of Blackcliff," she said, smile deepening as he straightened. A dimple danced at the corner of her mouth. Trevor found himself unable to look away.

The grandfather clock in the entryway chimed ten. "Oh, goodness! I've kept you from your appointment!" She seized Trevor's hand. "This way to the library. I'm sure my father has everything laid out to explain the estate to you."

Trevor didn't resist as she tugged him out of the withdrawing room and down the corridor. She had strong hands for a woman, sturdy, unlike his mother's long, elegant fingers. She was also the busiest woman he'd ever met. Everywhere he looked he saw evidence of her handiwork.

Windows that had been grimy with dust now sparkled in the golden light of autumn. Every last cobweb had been obliterated. She must have enlisted each man, woman and child in the village to clean the place and stood as their captain. And she didn't even look tired!

She threw open the door to the library with a flourish and stepped aside for him to enter. He thought surely she'd wait outside, perhaps even go straight to attack the cellar, but she followed him inside and shut the door behind her.

He had the oddest sense of a trap being sprung.

He glanced around the library, trying to determine what was wrong. Every wall was hidden by tall oak bookcases with leaded glass fronts. The only open space was for the paneled door by which he'd entered, the wide window opposite it overlooking the grounds and the black marble fireplace to his right. Candles in the brass chandelier cast down a glow on the stout leather-bound chairs scattered about the ruby-patterned carpet and the massive, claw-foot desk across the room.

This was where a gentleman conducted business—thoughtful, logical, impressive. For the first time, he began to feel at home.

An older man stood with his back to the desk, hands braced behind him on its surface as if he needed its strength. Where Gwen Allbridge was an all-consuming fire, her father looked more like a burned-out husk. His gray hair was thinning and receding, his cheeks hollowed. His body was too narrow for the plaid wool coat and brown breeches that hung from it.

He pushed off from the desk and managed a bow, his voice creaking out of him as if even breathing was a struggle. "Sir Trevor, an honor to meet you. Horace Allbridge at your service."

"Allbridge," Trevor greeted him, moving into the room. "I understand I have you to thank for keeping my estate safe."

His steward immediately dropped his gaze to his

scuffed brown boots and shuffled them against the carpet. "Only doing my duty, sir."

Trevor swung around him and seated himself at the desk. The black leather-bound armchair didn't offer a protest as he sank into it, fitting his frame as if it had been made for him. He rubbed his hands over the smooth desktop, saw his reflection gazing thoughtfully back at him in the polished surface. If he turned his head, he could gaze out at his garden and the black fell rising behind the house.

Something drifted over him, strong, sure. If he'd had to name it, he would have called it peace.

He took a breath and raised his head. Gwendolyn Allbridge was watching him from her place near the door. He'd seen similar smiles on the faces of new mothers, excessively proud of their babbling infants. But was it her father or him she found so adorable?

Not a little discomposed by the thought, he waved toward another of the leather-bound chairs on the other side of the desk. "Have a seat," he told her father. "I'd like a full report."

Allbridge perched on the edge of the chair, spine inches away from the back of it. He blinked bleary blue eyes as if trying in vain to gather his thoughts.

Gwen seemed to sense it. Her smile faded, and she hurried closer. "I'm sure you have a great deal to report, Father," she said, for all the world like a teacher coaxing a student to answer a difficult question.

Did the man need such help? What kind of steward was he that he required his daughter's prompting to do his duty? Trevor had assumed the man had been working at her side all night; now he could only wonder.

"Miss Allbridge," he said, giving her his most charming smile. "Forgive us for taking up your time. I'm certain you have other matters on your mind this fine day."

She came forward eagerly, face alight. "Not at all! I love hearing how well Blackcliff is doing!"

Her father cleared his throat with a phlegmy rattle. "Could take some time. Best you see to Sir Trevor's tea. Wouldn't want him to perish of thirst, now, would we?"

Her face fell, but she nodded. "Of course. I'll be right back." She hurried from the room.

"Your daughter is a credit to you, sir," Trevor said.

"That she is," Gwen's father agreed. "She's been managing Blackcliff for years." He glanced after her as if to make sure she'd shut the door behind her, then scooted forward on his chair until Trevor thought he'd surely fall flat on the floor.

He raised his gaze to meet Trevor's. "Unfortunately, I have no good news to tell you about Blackcliff, sir, and that's the truth of it."

Trevor felt as if the room had darkened. "As bad as all that?"

Allbridge nodded solemnly. "The estate has no income to speak of and any attempt to rectify that will incur a princely sum. Unless you've a pretty penny in your pocket, you might as well ride for London this very afternoon and thank the good Lord that no more of the place rubbed off on you."

Chapter Five

Trevor stood at the library window, staring out at the estate. A shelf of green lawn led up to the base of Blackcliff Fell. Rob Winslow walked past, leading Icarus, who dropped his head to nibble at the grass. Clouds floated serenely in the blue sky. It was as bucolic a scene as he might have wished for as the new lord of the manor. But it was a lie.

After his steward's pessimistic assessment, Trevor had pressed him for details. All had been bleak. Most estates Trevor knew had a thousand acres or more, much of them good pastureland for sheep or cattle, or fields for crops of one kind or another. All those lands needed was a set of tenants with half Miss Allbridge's energy to bring in a handsome income that allowed their owners to live in luxury, most often in London.

The Blackcliff estate had only a few hundred acres, the vast majority taken up by that hulking rocky mountain. Blackcliff Fell didn't offer enough pasture for more than the most hardy of sheep. There were no tenant farmers; there was nowhere for them to farm. As the owner of the land on which the village and church sat, Trevor received rent from each cottage and shop, based on the yearly income. Unfortunately, with the mine closed, there was precious little income to be had.

"But you claim the mine was prosperous," Trevor had said, trying to keep the frustration from his voice. "Why shut it down?"

"It wore out," Allbridge had said in his rusty voice. Trevor wasn't sure if his accompanying sigh was for the situation or Trevor's question. "We even had a man killed from falling rock. That fall buried the biggest vein of wad."

Trevor frowned. Why couldn't it have been gold or silver? "Wad? Is that what we mine?"

"Aye, sir. Was used to cast His Majesty's cannons, I hear. Now they use it to fill pencils."

The fellow must mean graphite. Trevor had heard it came principally from Cumberland. "What's the market?"

"Generally good. The mines at Borrowdale can only produce so much. Seems there's always more demand."

A demand he couldn't meet with a mine too dangerous to work. "Why did the villagers act as if it were my decision to reopen the mine?" he pressed.

"People will do most anything to feed their families," his steward had replied. "They didn't want to believe the surveyors the colonel had in." He'd cast Trevor a sidelong look that made Trevor think of his daughter. "I suppose the villagers were hoping you were the type of gentleman who was willing to invest in his mine."

He'd have been more than happy to invest, if he'd had a penny to spare. He had plans for the income this estate should have produced—a house, a carriage, a wife of noble birth and decent marriage settlements, a place among good Society, respected, admired.

"I'd like to read the surveyor's report," he'd told his steward, but it had not been among the records Allbridge had brought for Trevor's perusal. His steward had promised to locate it as soon as possible.

Until then, Gwen's father had recommended that Trevor look over his estate. Allbridge made it sound as if Trevor might discover something worthwhile, something valuable that would make him wish to stay. What man in his right mind stayed on a lifeless rock?

"You haven't tasted your tea."

He turned at the sound of Gwen Allbridge's warm voice. She was standing in the doorway, her fiery hair the one spot of brightness in the room. She'd taken off her green coat and wore a white apron over her green-checked cotton gown. She looked industrious and competent. He felt neither.

His feelings must have shown on his face, despite his best intentions, for her brows rose, and she hurried into the room.

"What's wrong?" she demanded. "Was the tea not to your liking? Mrs. Bentley thought you'd favor the souchong but that smoky smell isn't for everyone. Or did we miss a spot when we were cleaning?"

Trevor forced a smile for her sake. "I wasn't thirsty, after all, and the house seems immaculate. You almost make me believe in miracles."

"Almost?" she teased, cocking her head and endangering the pile of curls on top.

He felt his smile slipping and returned his gaze to the black, unforgiving mountain. "I had hoped for better news from your father."

He heard her suck in a breath, then the rustle of skirts as she hurried around in front of him.

Her brown eyes were imploring. "He hasn't had to give a report in months. I'm sure if you allow him a little time, he'll do better."

She seemed to take it personally that anything might not be to his liking. "You mistake me," he assured her. "I find no fault in your father. He came straight to the point, a trait I admire."

"Then what?" she begged.

He could not stop looking at that mountain. It dwarfed the house; it blighted his hopes. "I simply could not like the truth."

She angled her head to look up into his eyes. "The truth? That the village is overjoyed you're here? That you have a venerable home you can be proud of? That you will make an excellent master for Blackcliff? How can you not like those truths?"

"They were not truths I expected," he replied. In the face of her optimism he was beginning to feel like a spoiled child. Yet she could not know how important wealth and consequence were in his world. "There is nothing for me here."

Her eyes widened as if in shock, and she drew herself up, once more all righteousness. "Nothing? What nonsense! You, sir, are coming with me." She strode for the door, and he turned to watch her, surprised by the sudden change.

"I'll ask Mrs. Bentley to fetch your coat," she threw back over her shoulder. "We're going for a walk, and then, sir, we will see about this nothing!"

She was out the door before he could argue. But then, he doubted she'd have listened if he'd tried.

Nothing? How could he call Blackcliff nothing? Blackcliff was her home; Blackcliff was her world. More, it was the world of every man, woman and child in the village, and it had been for generations. He should be happy to be welcomed, stranger that he was. He should be overjoyed to learn what he'd been given here.

"But wasn't he pleased?" Mrs. Bentley asked, following Gwen back to the library with Sir Trevor's coat bundled in her arms. Gwen had found her in the butler's pantry, a small room just off the dining room that held the china and silver service and served as a place to keep the food warm after it had been carried from the kitchen in the outbuilding. "Does he approve of what we've done with the house?"

"He will," Gwen promised, pulling on her own green coat and cinching the ribbon under her breast. "Just give me a day."

"I'll be happy to give you all the time you need, dearie," the little housekeeper replied with a sad smile. "I really have nowhere else to go."

Neither did Gwen and her father. She'd lived her entire life in that gatehouse. Her mother had married, given birth and died there. Her father was only now beginning to find himself again after her death. Blackcliff Hall, Blackcliff village, St. Martin's Church—they were all Gwen had ever known. Leaving was unthinkable. The very idea robbed her of speech, set her stomach to cramping.

Oh, but Sir Trevor had to be made to see reason! This house was their last chance to keep the village together in the coming years. A great house had hunting parties in the autumn, Christmas parties in the winter and house parties in the spring and summer. Visitors toured the area, ordered food from the George, bought laces and writing paper and gloves from the village shops, left money to thank the servants.

A great house had gardens that needed tending, horses to care for, carriages to manage. It needed maids and footmen and cooks, perhaps even a governess and nursemaid if the master's family was increasing. Blackcliff would keep them all together.

But only if Sir Trevor was happy enough with the place to make it his home.

Why had her father emphasized the negative? A shame she couldn't have stayed while he had made his report. She could have corrected mistakes, shown Blackcliff in a better light. She knew how to manage the estate; she'd followed her father about his duties since she was a child, taking on more of a role each year as her father and Colonel Umbrey aged.

But even if she had stayed with her father this morning, she knew she had to be careful how much she helped him. He needed to feel useful; he needed to take back his place in the community. Surely that would get him over this depression he continued to fight. Right now, though, she just had to make sure his dismal report didn't affect her plans for Blackcliff.

She marched into the library, prepared to counter any argument Sir Trevor might mount, but he came around the desk to meet her and Mrs. Bentley with a polite smile. He even bent over backward to allow the little housekeeper to shrug him into his greatcoat.

"Is there something special I can cook you for dinner, then, sir?" she asked as he straightened, her big brown eyes looking up into his.

He adjusted his coat across his broad shoulders. "I'm sure whatever you have will be fine, Mrs. Bentley."

She nodded, then leaned toward Gwen. "The salmon, I think," she whispered. "And pudding. I don't know a man who doesn't like pudding."

Gwen could only hope the housekeeper was right. At the moment, it seemed that Sir Trevor liked little about Blackcliff. But she was about to change all that.

Please, Lord, let me change all that!

"If you'd be so kind as to follow me, Sir Trevor," she said, then held her breath.

But he nodded, motioning her out the door ahead of him.

Emboldened, Gwen led him through the manor and onto the lawn before the fell.

How could he fail to appreciate the view? Gwen loved autumn at Blackcliff. The cool air was moist and tangy. The black rock made the fiery rowans and oaks and the russet ash stand out in sharp relief. With so much color, the ugly charcoal-colored piles of wad tailings around the mouth of the mine half-way up the slope were barely noticeable.

She paused, turning to him. "You like to ride, don't you?"

He raised a brow as if he hadn't expected the question. "Indeed."

She pointed along the foot of the fell. "There's an excellent path along there. If you head west, it will take you to the top of the dale. East will lead you down the dale into the Lockhart estate. The squire and his son are bruising riders, too. I'm sure they wouldn't mind you jumping a few fences."

"At least they have fences," he replied.

So much for riding. *Lord, guide my words! Show me what he'd find good here!*

Then a verse came to her mind: *Come, and let us go up to the mountain of the Lord.*

The mountain! Of course. "And you have Black-cliff," she replied, turning to head for the well-worn footpath up the fell. "This way."

"This isn't necessary," he said, though she felt him behind her.

"It is entirely necessary," she insisted, lifting her skirts to clamber up the rocky path. Behind her came a thud and a grunt, and she turned to find him on one knee, sliding backward on the rocks. She reached out a hand and grabbed his coat, slowing him. Oh, but he was a solid fellow! She teetered on the rock, perilously close to falling herself. *Lord, help me!*

Her gaze met his and, for a moment, she thought her panic had infected him, as well. Then his eyes narrowed as if in determination, and he surged upward, caught her and pulled her into the safety of his arms. Gwen stood, wrapped in his embrace, her chest against his ribs, blinking up at him.

"I can see why you thought this would improve

my perception of Blackcliff," he said, gazing down at her. His mouth curved up in a smile.

Heat flushed up her, and she disengaged from him. "Actually, you'll find the view from the top is much better."

His smile turned sad. "You're wasting your time, I fear."

"Then I shall apologize sweetly for taking you out of your way," Gwen replied. But she started resolutely upward once more and heard the rocks rattle under his boots as he followed.

They climbed in silence for a while, the sounds of their footfalls quieted by the still air. The brambles along the path were turning a peachy orange, their berries almost as dark as the ground. Did he appreciate the show? A falcon soared by, nearly eye level with them. Did he see its majesty?

Apparently not, for he asked, "Why do you stay? Why do any of you stay?"

A simple enough question, for Gwen. "It's home," she told him, breath starting to come in pants. "My father's here. My friends are here. But there's more to it than that. You'll see in a moment."

With a last push, she reached the top. Sharp slabs of shale lay piled on the ground like dirty dishes on a footman's tray. The air was cool and just as sharp, stinging her cheeks, tugging at her curls, whistling as it passed. Trevor drew up beside her, standing tall into the blue, blue sky.

Gwen spread her arms and turned in a circle.

"Look around you, Sir Trevor. Everything you see is yours."

He turned slowly, eyes widening. The crimson of autumn gave way to the white of new snow on the upper peaks in the distance. They had only a dusting now, like sugar on cinnamon loaves, but they'd be all white before winter's end. Their forested sides ran down to clear brooks and wide fields. Gwen linked one arm with his and pointed with the other.

"Your land extends to the top of the next peak. See that stream in the valley between the two? It's filled with salmon. You'll have some for dinner tonight."

He nodded as if the idea had merit.

Encouraged, she tugged him to the north. "See that copse of trees? That's yours, too. You'll find deer and fox and ermine and plenty of wood for your fire."

One corner of his mouth curved upward. Ah, perhaps he liked to hunt. She could use that to her advantage.

She turned him east, and the whole of the Evendale Valley spread out, the village a set of small white squares against the green. "You see those cottages, those shops? Those are your people, your neighbors. They rely on you to provide opportunities for income and advancement. You can rely on them for friendship and service in good times and comfort in bad."

His half smile disappeared.

What was wrong with him? Why couldn't he see what Blackcliff had to offer?

She released his arm and put both hands on her hips. "Come now, Sir Trevor Fitzwilliam of Blackcliff. How can you call this nothing?"

Chapter Six

How could Trevor explain? He could see the beauty of the place—wild, untrammeled. He could imagine riding Icarus along those narrow paths, hunting in the shaded woods, fishing in the crystal streams. If he'd wanted no more than a warm fire, good food and loyal companions, Blackcliff would have satisfied. But he wanted more. Blackcliff might be Gwen Allbridge's world, but his was bigger and hundreds of miles away.

Still, she regarded him, feathery brows up, slender body poised, waiting for him to agree with her assessment, to offer praise.

The best he could do was smile. "I never meant to denigrate your home. It's a fine estate and a lovely village. It's simply not what I planned."

She cocked her head, and the cold mountain air whipped a coppery strand of hair across her face. "What did you plan?"

He gazed off over the fells, shadows against the blue sky. "Farmland, tenants." He snorted. "At the very least an orchard or two."

She straightened and shrugged as if those did not seem so important to her. "You'll find some of that in the lower valley, but it's too rocky here for more than a small garden."

"So I've noticed."

She waved her hand, sweeping away his concerns. "There are far more interesting things here in any event."

Trevor eyed her. "Such as?"

She raised her chin. "We have a fine church. St. Martin's was built in the thirteenth century, you know."

So even his church was old and no doubt needed work. "A venerable establishment, to be sure."

She laughed. "Your words are praising, sir, but I see the look in your eyes. Very well. I suppose St. Martin's may not be all that interesting to someone of your sophistication. So, tell me, where would you prefer to live?"

"London," he readily replied.

This time he was the one expecting a quick agreement. London was the capital, the seat of government, the hub of commerce. Anyone who was anyone spent at least part of the year in London.

To his surprise, she wrinkled her nose. "London? Why? You must see that Blackcliff is far and away superior."

Trevor raised a brow. "And on what do you base such a sweeping statement? Have you ever visited London?"

"Once," she admitted with a shudder that set the pink ribbon on her long green coat to shaking. "Mother went up to see a cousin who was being presented, and I accompanied her. And that was quite enough, I assure you. The air is filled with that nasty soot, carriages clog the roads, street vendors wake you in the wee hours to shout about milk and posies. No, thank you!"

With the exception of the soot from the coal fires, he found those things more interesting than irksome. "And were you given no opportunity to experience the culture? London boasts lofty architecture, galleries of fine art and sculpture, exceptional dressmakers and expert tailors."

"Ah, shopping," she said wisely. "Come with me to Blackcliff village, sir, and see if you don't find it equally diverting."

He'd seen enough of the little village riding through it last night and today. The entire collection of buildings could be hidden in one corner of London, and no one would notice. Instead of looking at aged churches, he should be in the library, reading documents, checking calculations. He had to decide what to do about Blackcliff, determine how soon he could head back to London. "I'm sure the village is delightful, but I'm certain your father would prefer that I return to the manor."

He thought surely she'd agree with that. She'd been quick to support her father on every other occasion. Instead, she shook her head doggedly.

"But you can't hide away in Blackcliff Hall," she urged, taking a step closer as if to make her case. The scent of roses drifted toward him on the breeze. "The most important men in the village wish to meet you."

She knew how to flatter his vanity, he'd give her that. Some part of him felt smugly pleased that the local men would want to meet him, perhaps seek his counsel. But why bother even making their acquaintance if he wasn't going to stay?

She must have seen his hesitation, for she slipped her hand into his and smiled up at him. "You could ride Icarus," she said as if offering a bribe to a recalcitrant child.

He chuckled. "I could ride Icarus back to London, as well."

She pulled free. "Yes, you could, but you'd miss all the fun. I'll meet you at the bottom." She lifted her cotton skirts above the tops of her boots and started down the slope, as graceful as a bird skimming the clouds.

With a last look at his empty land, Trevor turned and followed.

He did not ride Icarus, though she paused by the stables expectantly. A gentleman didn't ride while a lady walked. He'd only done so this morning because of the village procession. When Trevor made no move to call for Rob Winslow to saddle his horse, she led him around the side of the house, across the front garden and through a side gate onto a pebbled footpath.

"You see?" she said as she shut the iron gate behind him. "You even have your own private entrance to the village." She nodded to where a stone bridge arched over a narrow stream that bubbled along a rocky trough among ashes and oaks. "This will bring you out right next to the George. And you couldn't ask for a more beautiful route."

With autumn leaves drifting down across the clear water, the path was a picturesque sight. Yet so were the horse races at Ascot on opening day, each mount groomed to a sheen, every lady poised and polished as she watched, every gentleman eager for the outcome of the races.

"You are well versed in the beauties of Blackcliff," Trevor said as they crossed the bridge and headed for the inn. "However, you must admit that the village lacks some of the amenities one might expect of a city like London."

She frowned. "Such as?"

"No gentlemen's clubs," he suggested.

"I'm certain you will never lack for manly company at the George," she countered. They were passing the establishment now, and she waved to Mrs. Billings, who was out on the front steps haggling with a farmer over a wagon full of milk cans. "Besides, do you ever truly know the members of your club? Would they stick by you through thick and thin?"

She had a point. The members of White's had voted on three separate occasions before agreeing to admit him to London's most famous gentlemen's club, and he still didn't feel welcome. But going to a club was as much about being seen in the right circles as it was about making friends.

"Still," Trevor said, "you have no daily news."

"Just ask Mrs. Bentley," she replied, skirting the inn and starting up the lane that led to the other end of the village. "She keeps up with everyone."

He imagined she might, more quickly and with less rancor than *The Times*. "But no balls or routs."

She cast him a quick glance. "We have a lovely assembly in the market hall every quarter. The next one is only two weeks away."

She had an answer for everything, it seemed. "Yet no opportunity to participate in government," he finished, certain she'd have no answer for that. Parliament, after all, was in London.

She shook her head solemnly. "I fear, Sir Trevor, that you will have no end of opportunity to participate in government. And we should start with David Newton, immediately."

He was ready to ask who this Newton fellow might be when he realized where she was leading him. A bell tower rose over the cottages and trees, a cross etched in its side.

St. Martin's Church was a long building with the

three-story tower at one end and a two-story chapel on the other. While the tower had been white-washed, the stones of the rest of the church were dark; lichen and old moss speckled them gray and green. Only a few narrow and clear leaded-glass windows broke up the expanse of wall. Gravestones poked up at odd angles among the rough-trimmed grass of the churchyard, and wind moaned under the pitched eaves. He imagined it wasn't hard to ponder a dismal eternity in such a place.

The vicarage was just as cheerless, being a square gray box of a building set off to one side. A plain-faced woman with honey-colored hair sleeked back in a bun opened the door to Gwen's knock. Her brows shot up over her slate-gray eyes.

"Good morning, Ruth," Gwen said, moving into the long central corridor of the vicarage as if well acquainted with the shadowed place. "May I present Sir Trevor Fitzwilliam? He's the new owner of Blackcliff. Sir Trevor, Miss Ruth Newton."

Trevor bowed as Miss Newton turned scarlet and murmured her delight in meeting him. Gwen, how-ever, wandered down the corridor, peering in this room and that. She turned to her red-faced friend with a puzzled smile. "Where's your brother? I know he wanted to meet Sir Trevor."

Ruth Newton managed to close the door behind Trevor and smoothed down her charcoal-colored skirts with one hand. Of the local women Trevor had met, she was by far the best dressed. The high waist and straight fall of the elegant gown might have come from a London modiste.

"He had to see to Mrs. Wheaton this morning," she murmured. "Her youngest isn't doing well. Croup again."

Immediately Gwen's face fell, and she hurried back. "I'll send some of Mother's syrup straight away."

Ruth Newton sagged as if a burden had been lifted. "Oh, thank you, Miss Allbridge. I'm certain that would make all the difference."

"Of course!" She reached out and squeezed her friend's hand. "And how many times have I asked you to call me Gwen?"

The woman's gaze darted to Trevor, then fell. "I'm sure I should not be so familiar."

"Nonsense," Gwen said, releasing her. "Now be a dear and find some of your famous sweet buns. I'm certain Sir Trevor must be famished from all this walking."

Trevor tried to demur, but Miss Newton hurried off to the kitchen as if glad for an escape, and Gwen drew him into the cozy sitting room and directed him toward a comfortable upholstered chair by the fire. The worn arms and sagging seat told him others had warmed themselves here. It ought to feel shabby, yet he found himself leaning back with a sigh approaching contentment.

He thought she meant to sit, as well, but she waved a hand to tell him to keep his seat, then went to pick up a small table and move it across the room to his side. "Ruth is one of the best cooks in the upper valley," she confided. "She's also an expert with the needle. She makes all her own clothes and gives the rest of us advice, as well."

Was she trying to match him up with the woman? As the sister of the local minister and keeper of his house, Ruth Newton probably had the respect of the village. But Trevor had no interest in a woman so self-effacing she couldn't stand her ground in her own home.

Of course, he was beginning to realize, it would take a stronger will than his to withstand Gwen's determination.

"You mustn't praise me so," Ruth Newton protested as she carried a wooden tray into the room. She hesitated only a moment as if surprised to find her furniture rearranged, then set the tray on the table beside Trevor. "Sir Trevor will think I take on airs. Tea, Sir Trevor?"

Her hand hovered over the china teapot patterned in red roses, and she and Gwen watched him expectantly. What was so significant about a cup of tea? Another time he might have graciously refused, but the walk had made him thirsty.

"Certainly," he said, and Ruth Newton took a deep breath and set about pouring.

"Ruth and her brother arrived here three years ago," Gwen supplied, accepting a cup from her friend. "Our last minister served for thirty years."

That had to have seemed endless in this place, but then he supposed most ministers hoped for such a tenure. "Admirable."

"We are very grateful for the living," Miss Newton put in, fingers gripping her cup. She swallowed even though Trevor was certain she hadn't taken a sip yet. "Not that we didn't have choices. David did very well at Oxford, you understand."

"We are fortunate to have him," Gwen put in loyally. She scooted to the edge of her seat just as her father had done and reached out to pick up the plate of buns from the tea tray and offer it to Trevor.

"Try one," she urged. "They're sublime."

He wasn't hungry, but they were both watching him again. So, he picked up a bun and made a show of taking a bite. The pastry was buttery and flaky, the center flavored with almonds.

He smiled as he swallowed. "They are excellent. My compliments, Miss Newton."

She blushed again, but Gwen sat back in her chair and grinned as if well satisfied with herself.

Down the corridor came the sound of a door opening and closing, then the thump of boots hurrying toward them. A slender man of medium height with wind-tossed brown hair and a bottle nose strode into the room. His gray eyes were wide and not a little panicked.

"Sir Trevor! I came as soon as I could." He extended his right hand while trying to push back his hair with the other.

Trevor rose and shook his hand. "Mr. Newton, a pleasure. And no need for concern. Your charming sister has kept me company. You are fortunate to have such a talented sibling."

"Talented?" He glanced at his sister as if he'd never seen her before.

Ruth Newton raised her chin. "Sir Trevor enjoyed my sweet buns."

"Oh." The minister laughed nervously. "Of course. They are a favorite in the village." He sobered. "But you mustn't think we pride ourselves on them, Sir Trevor. Pride goeth before a fall, as I'm sure you know." He glanced about as if for support, and his sister nodded gravely.

"I'm sure Sir Trevor understands," Gwen said with a comforting smile. "And how is little Tim Wheaton?"

Newton's shoulders slumped, and he sighed. "Not well. The other children haven't come down with it, thank God, but he coughs so hard, so often, I daresay the rest of the household isn't getting much sleep. I thought of your mother's horehound syrup, but I didn't know how much you had left." He glanced at Trevor as if suspecting he had need of it.

"I've a spare bottle," Gwen said. "I'll send it round as soon as we return to the Hall. And I'll check on them later."

Care coiled around the room, like fine perfume, embracing her and the Newtons. If he stayed, would it reach him, too? He was surprised to feel the prick of longing.

The minister thanked her, then returned his gaze to Trevor. "I suppose you have questions for me. I've a curriculum vitae, recommendations from my tutors at Oxford and a copy of some of my better sermons. You understand, of course, that only the bishop can take me from the living, what with Colonel Umbrey placing me here." His laugh was once more nervous.

Ah, so that was it. The position of vicar of St. Martin's must be appointed by the master of the Blackcliff estate. Trevor had heard that some landowners even managed to have prospective ministers pay a sum for the privilege. It seemed that too was denied him.

But he knew what was expected of him. He drew himself up, gazing down at the minister, whose shoulders sagged farther.

"I have no plans to complain to the bishop about your place, Vicar," Trevor assured him. "Your credentials and standing in this community are impressive. I have heard nothing but praise for your work. I know I speak for the entire village when I say I wish you many productive years here at Blackcliff."

If only he could say the same about himself.

Chapter Seven

Goodness, but Sir Trevor was impressive. Gwen thought if he'd looked at her the way he was regarding David Newton, she might have found a way to fly to the moon and back, if it pleased him. David Newton must have felt the same way, for he seized Sir Trevor's hand and shook it over and over, while Ruth wiped at her eyes and murmured thanks.

Sir Trevor continued a polite conversation as he strolled toward the door, asking about the number of baptisms, marriages and funerals performed in the past year; evincing interest in a scheme to refinish the pews. Before Gwen knew it, they were out the door and back on the lane into the village. Only then did he turn to her with a raised brow.

"You might have warned me."

Gwen frowned. "About what? You were wonderful in there."

He sighed. "Thank you, but it would have helped

to know that the living at St. Martin's belongs to the Blackcliff estate."

"Surely they told you," Gwen protested.

He rubbed the bridge of his nose as if he felt a headache coming on. "No, Miss Allbridge, I assure you. No one told me anything about Blackcliff except its general direction."

How extraordinary! She certainly wouldn't have presumed to take up residence halfway across the country without knowing a great deal about the place first. But then, she wouldn't have left Blackcliff no matter what was promised elsewhere.

"Is there anything else I should know?" he asked as they headed back through the village.

He sounded so weary she almost hated to tell him. "The village elects the constable, the church warden, the surveyor of highways and the overseer of the poor, but as the master of Blackcliff, everyone expects you to voice your support."

"Let's get this over with," he gritted out, and Gwen directed him forward once more.

For the next hour, she led Sir Trevor from place to place in the village. The constable, Mr. Casperson, who owned one of the shops, stood with both his chins held high while he expounded his views regarding vagrancy to Sir Trevor. The church warden, Mr. Williamson, pledged his undying devotion to Blackcliff and assured Sir Trevor that he would take good care of the church and its people. Rob Winslow's father, who served as surveyor, saluted the baronet with an iron bar.

And Mr. Agnew grew positively teary-eyed in telling Sir Trevor what an honor it was to oversee the poor.

"And I know we will have fewer on the rolls now that Blackcliff Mine is to be opened," the wheelwright said with a tremulous smile as they stood before the whitewashed stone building where he made and repaired the village wagons.

Gwen glanced at Sir Trevor, but he merely returned the smile, and with far greater strength. She could not allow this story to continue. False hope, once dashed, was more demoralizing than no hope at all.

"I fear there was a misunderstanding," she told the gray-haired man. "Blackcliff Mine is too dangerous to be reopened." She lay a hand on his muscular shoulder, the leather of his apron firm against her palm. "I'm very sorry."

Mr. Agnew blinked. "But I heard it from Mrs. Dennings."

Sir Trevor stepped closer, forcing Gwen to drop her hand. "Ah, such a charming woman, Mrs. Dennings. Her husband worked at the mine, I believe."

How did he know? Gwen hadn't told him, and she doubted her father's account had included the names of every miner. He must have pieced together the story from stray facts.

Mr. Agnew nodded, shifting on his booted feet as

if he longed to go back inside his shop and work on something simple like a wagon wheel. "Jack Dennings was a good man. When he was killed during a cave-in, the colonel thought it best to close things up. But Jack Dennings wasn't the only man put out of work that day." He frowned up at Sir Trevor.

"I share your assessment on the importance of the mine," Trevor said. His look to Gwen held a request for silence. "When I spoke this morning, I was unaware of the state of decay. I intend to learn more, and I will do everything I can to keep my promise."

Mr. Agnew's wrinkled face beamed. "Well, certainly. And we will all look forward to good news for Blackcliff."

"And there we quite agree," Gwen said, but she took Sir Trevor's arm and nudged him away from the wheelwright. It was like trying to push a stone wall. She was glad he didn't resist as she led him toward the Hall at last.

"You shouldn't encourage them," Gwen said as they headed for the main gates. "Did my father explain the situation?"

"He did, but I have yet to read the surveyor's report." His strides were lengthening, as if he couldn't wait to leave the village behind.

Gwen wrinkled her nose even as she hurried her steps to keep pace. "I have read it. The mine is a ruin."

As soon as the words left her mouth she wanted to call them back. She sounded as dismal as her father. She forced a smile and scurried around in front of him.

"But who needs a mine?" she asked as the familiar iron gates loomed. "Blackcliff has always taken care of itself. I'm sure it will be no different with you."

"Your confidence is inspiring," he said, but she thought she heard an edge to his otherwise polite voice.

"You were very kind to confirm all those positions," she replied, trying to remind him of the esteem in which the master of Blackcliff was held. "Everyone will breathe easier now that you've shown yourself happy with their appointments."

"I live to serve."

Still no warmth underlay that cultured voice. She could not conceive she had tired him. Those long legs looked made for striding about, the dove-gray pantaloons molded to his muscles. She tore her gaze away.

"So, what else would you like to do today?" she asked.

He stopped so suddenly she nearly tripped. His face was still that polite mask, all calm and considerate, but she could not name the emotion that crouched in his green gaze.

"There is nothing else I could want from today, Miss Allbridge," he said, voice tightly controlled. "I think you have accomplished quite enough. My home is overrun with people I cannot hope to pay.

My boots are scuffed from climbing a mountain I wish I'd never seen. My honor is strained by supporting men in positions I have no idea whether they can fulfill. And by sundown a good portion of the village will think that I lied about opening the mine. All in all, it has been a full day, and the only thing I wish right now is to be left alone."

He swept her a bow and stalked up the drive for the house.

Gwen stared after his retreating figure. What was wrong with him? She'd shown him that his land contained the top of the world, which ought to make any man feel proud. She'd shown him that he had influence over the lives of other people, which ought to make him humbly grateful or smugly self-satisfied, depending on the type of gentleman he was.

But Sir Trevor didn't seem proud or grateful or even slightly satisfied. He sounded frustrated beyond all endurance!

He seemed to think she'd terribly inconvenienced him when she'd done everything for his convenience. Would he have preferred to spend the night mopping floors or making beds? Would he have rather spent the day moping at the library window instead of doing something good for himself and the village? What sort of man had been given control of their lives?

She started for the gatehouse, ribbon on her coat swishing from side to side in her agitation. *Talk to him, Lord. Help him see what You've given him here. Help him live up to his new responsibilities.*

Immediately a thought came to her, something her father had once said: *Sometimes you have to walk before you can run.* She frowned as she let herself into the gatehouse. Was that Sir Trevor's dilemma? Was he so new at his role he truly didn't understand how much he was needed?

The sitting room was empty, but she knew her father must be in the house. A fire glowed in the stone fireplace, shedding light on the square-backed upholstered chairs on either side. An earlier mistress of Blackcliff had been displeased with the basket-of-flowers pattern woven into the emerald fabric and the dark curve of the polished legs. She had consigned the pieces to the gatehouse.

Gwen's mother had called them the thrones. They were a little grand next to the whitewashed walls and simple half-moon table where Gwen and her father usually ate. But then, Gwen supposed, that was the way of the stewards of Blackcliff: expected to be more than a servant but less than the master.

Her father was in the kitchen, cutting a thick slice of bread for himself at the solid worktable in the center of the room. Dolly lay at his feet, big head on her paws, jowls brushing the stone floor. She looked relaxed, but her eyes followed his every move.

"How did it go in the village?" he asked before taking a big bite.

Gwen made a face. "All the elected positions

have been confirmed, but it seems Sir Trevor did not enjoy the process." She crossed to where hooks by the back door held her father's coat and pulled off her own. "What do you know of him, Father?"

He shrugged. "Not much. You were the one who saw his papers."

She had, but she hadn't noticed anything odd. "I originally assumed this was only one of his many properties," she said, taking down her apron and wrapping it about her gown. "That he was used to overseeing the lives of his tenants. But his papers said he'd been given the estate for services to the Crown. What if he's never owned property before? What if he has no idea what he's doing?"

Her father tore off another bite of the bread. Dolly sighed heavily. "Seems like a smart fellow," he said. "Likely he could learn."

The master of Blackcliff, learning how to lead? She ought to panic. They needed someone who was stronger. Colonel Umbrey had come from a long line of masters of Blackcliff and look at the damage he'd done: shutting down the mine with no thought of the consequences, his callous treatment of his staff, his incessant fears at the end, sure someone was out to harm him. Was having someone who knew nothing any better?

It had to be!

She walked to the pantry that ran under the stairs and opened the door. The light from the kitchen window spilled over bottles and jars of pure white, deep purple and fiery crimson: her mother's treasures, neatly lined up on the shelves, waiting for her to return. But she wouldn't be returning. Gwen couldn't make herself step inside.

"He'll need help," she tossed back to her father over her shoulder instead. "We'll need to show him what it means to be the master of Blackcliff and the leader of the upper valley."

Her father swallowed the last of the bread, and Dolly closed her eyes as if giving up on him. "Only if he decides to stay."

Gwen faced the pantry. "He has to stay."

Her father followed her to the door and glanced inside with a sigh. "What do you need, daughter?"

"The horehound syrup. Tim Wheaton is ailing again."

Her father stepped inside and drew down the clear bottle. "Last one," he said, handing it to Gwen with gentle fingers. "She left you the recipe, you know. Likely you could make some before frost comes."

"Perhaps," Gwen said, backing away from the room and the memories it held with the bottles of preserves and cures.

Her father sighed as he closed the door behind him. "You like him, then, this Sir Trevor? You want him to stay?"

She felt her face heating and busied herself finding a cloth and wrapping the bottle. "Of course I want him to stay. You'll have your old position back. The village will have a source of income."

"He's a handsome fellow," her father said, leaning against the doorjamb between the kitchen and the sitting room. "I've no doubt you wouldn't be the first to notice."

Gwen smiled as she turned to him. "Ruth Newton turned positively crimson, the poor dear."

"More likely the other girls will turn green knowing you've already set your cap for him."

"I've done no such thing," Gwen said primly, setting the wrapped bottle in her work basket. "I've no interest in a man with leanings outside this valley. I'm needed here."

He grimaced as he straightened. "I haven't had more than my share of the cups in three months, and you know it."

She crossed to his side and kissed him on the cheek. "And is that the only reason you need me, to keep the gin out of reach?"

He glanced at her out of the corners of his blue eyes. "You know I dote on you. But there's a whole world outside this village. Perhaps it's time we saw it."

Fear wrapped around her, drew her tight. Leave Blackcliff? Leave everything she'd ever known? Go somewhere she had no control over her own life? How could he even suggest it? "No, thank you, Father. This is my home. I have no wish to live anywhere else, not even to marry as fine a fellow as Sir Trevor."

* * *

Trevor regretted snapping at Gwen the moment she had turned and stomped off for the gatehouse. She was only trying to help him settle in. It was clear she wanted him to feel a part of the village.

But it was equally clear to Trevor that he would never fit in. A happy sinner like Trevor approve of the vicar's position like some pompous archbishop? His acquaintances in London would laugh themselves sick if they knew.

His temporary gardeners were busy hacking his garden into submission, he saw as he approached the house. They paused to remove their caps and nod as he passed. His temporary maid was dusting the withdrawing room when he entered; she scurried out of his sight so as not to give offense. His temporary housekeeper helped him off with his coat, her smile warm and welcoming. They expected him to hire, to lead. They wanted a savior.

Trevor was no one's savior.

He took the stairs for his bedchamber two at a time. It was a fine room, with dark furnishings that may not have been fashionable but were well made and sturdy. In the tall wardrobe along one paneled wall, he located the bag he had brought with him on the saddle like one of the green-bag travelers who flocked to the mountains to rhapsodize over the scenery.

His meager belongings could be returned to the bag easily enough. By nightfall, Icarus could reach

Carlisle. Another four days easy riding could get Trevor to London. He could stay with friends. A few conversations should put him onto a problem or two that could line his pockets for the quarter.

Crossing for the bureau to retrieve his spare shirt, he nearly tripped over the statue.

Trevor pulled up and stared at it. Sitting calmly on the carpet, the little shepherd stared straight ahead, looking for his sheep. Who'd carried it up the stairs? Why put it in his bedchamber?

Are You trying to tell me something, Lord?

He recoiled at the thought. Why ask such a question, as if expecting an answer? God didn't speak to people like him, men of uncertain birth, consigned to the shadows. If his own father couldn't be bothered to speak to him directly, why would a heavenly Father care?

For I know the thoughts I think toward you, saith the Lord. Thoughts of peace and not calamity, to give you a future and a hope.

What an odd mood he was in to remember verses from the few times he'd attended church. Trevor carried the statue to the door and set it carefully along the wall in the corridor outside his bedchamber, where the ancient suits of armor stared down at it. His visit with the Newtons must have dredged up the memory of God's promise. And as for thoughts of peace, the Lord had to have an odd sense of humor if he saw any future or hope in Blackcliff.

Trevor returned to the room and eyed the worn

leather travel bag, sitting on the down coverlet of the bed. Could something be made from Blackcliff? The mine seemed the most likely possibility. He hadn't seen this surveyor's report yet. It might give him some ideas. And he wasn't the type of gentleman to run away from difficulties.

He sighed and returned the case to the wardrobe. He'd give Blackcliff a few more days, see what he could learn. With any luck, he could still leave by the end of the week, if not sooner.

He did not count on Gwen Allbridge giving him reasons to stay.

Chapter Eight

The very next day, before Trevor had even finished the excellent breakfast Mrs. Bentley cooked him with ham and coddled eggs and buttery rolls so light he thought they could reach the top of Blackcliff Fell on their own, Gwen Allbridge appeared in the doorway. She was not an unwelcome sight, with her satiny matte-brown coat cinched under her bosom, a smoky veil draping her pale straw bonnet and coppery curls peeking out from under the brim. Trevor smiled a greeting as he swallowed the roll.

She grinned back. "I thought you might like some company on the walk to services this morning."

The roll caught in his throat, and he grabbed the cup of tea beside him and gulped down the warmth. Services? She meant church?

"How thoughtful of you," he said, lowering the cup carefully to its pale bone china saucer, trying to think of a way to answer. "But I would not want to inconvenience you."

"It's no inconvenience," she promised. "I'm sure everyone will be eager to see the Blackcliff pew filled once more."

So he even had his own pew. And, of course, they'd notice if it went empty. As a gentleman, he should escort her. He offered her a polite smile and called for his coat.

He wasn't sure what to expect of St. Martin's at Blackcliff. He'd never found any comfort in church. He'd done his best to sleep through the required services at school. The few times he'd attended St. George's Hanover Square in London had been more for show than anything else. He'd wanted to prove he had a right to be there. He'd scarcely listened to the readings; he'd been casting covert glances at the wealthy parishioners, waiting for them to turn and notice him, wondering if they would throw him out.

But the good people of Blackcliff were the ones craning their necks and casting him glances when he took his place at the front of the chapel. St. Martin's was more welcoming inside than out. Pale stone arches held up the heavily beamed ceiling. The narrow windows let in rays of light that etched the dark wood pews with lines of gold. Warmth seemed to curl from the candles; compassion echoed in the upraised voices that chanted the proper replies to David Newton's lead. Again that feeling of peace stole over Trevor.

Yet he could not believe they would want him worshiping with them if they truly knew him. In fact, he was fairly certain that if he was unable to open the mine, he would be wise to mount Icarus and escape to Carlisle at the first opportunity.

He had exited to the churchyard, where many of the congregation were loitering to exchange greetings after service, when Gwen brought a gentleman to meet him. Squire Lockhart was a tall, rugged fellow, with silver hair and a growing paunch that stretched his fine paisley waistcoat.

"Determined to make your acquaintance," he assured Trevor, wringing Trevor's hand in his meaty grip.

"Squire Lockhart has an impressive estate beyond Blackcliff," Gwen explained. Her wide smile said she thought she'd brought something akin to an Eastern potentate to Trevor's side.

Trevor was used to moving in the highest circles, if only on the edges of their august lives. Meeting a squire with an estate, no matter how impressive, did not discomfort him.

"And do you spend the entire year on your estate?" Trevor asked.

"Generally," the squire allowed. "Though I expect I'll need to go up to London once my granddaughter is in long skirts. Best place to catch a husband, my dear wife used to say, God rest her soul."

Trevor eyed Gwen. Though he thought her cheeks had darkened inside her veiled bonnet, she kept her gaze on the squire. Nothing about the fellow discomfited her, either, but then Trevor thought not even his exalted father would have discomfited Gwen.

"And didn't you tell me, sir," she said to the squire now, "that you had an express purpose in wanting to meet Sir Trevor?"

The squire, who had tipped his tall hat to Ruth Newton as she passed, set it back on his head with a flourish and eyed Trevor congenially. "Indeed I did. We expect a large party up from London tomorrow for a week of hunting. Perhaps you'd care to join us."

He was expected to agree; both Gwen's eager look and the squire's inquisitive blue gaze said so. Trevor enjoyed a good hunt the same as the next fellow, but he wasn't sure he should raise Gwen's expectations any further. He wasn't going to stay; he couldn't afford to stay. Still, what was a day?

"You are too kind," Trevor said. "But won't your other guests mind a stranger joining them?"

"Not such a stranger," Lockhart insisted. "I spent twenty years in the navy before retiring to the family estate after my older brother passed on. Several of those who are coming could tell similar tales. My last berth was the *Pegasus* in the Caribbean."

His gaze met Trevor's, sharper suddenly, assessing. Trevor refused to let him see that he'd hit a vein. "I know little about the navy, I fear. I would only bore your guests. Perhaps another time."

He thought the squire might press him, but Lockhart allowed the conversation to wander into predictions of harvest and the weather for the upcoming winter and commonplaces far less troubling than the name of the ship Trevor's father had captained. He was merely thankful the squire was a gentleman and would not demand that Trevor act in kind.

Gwen was highly tempted to stomp her foot or utter a shriek to voice her frustration. Unfortunately, St. Martin's churchyard was no place for such dramatic demonstrations of pique.

Yet how could she remain calm? Squire Lockhart was as close to royalty as she knew in the upper valley—a retired captain of the Royal Navy with friends in high places and a prominent landowner with an estate to rival Blackcliff. Sir Trevor should be delighted to make his acquaintance, to be rubbing shoulders with him and his London guests.

But she'd seen the moment Sir Trevor's face had tightened into that mask of politeness that snuffed all character. His reaction had something to do with the navy. He claimed he hadn't served in the army, that he'd found some administrative error to earn his baronetcy. Had it something to do with the HMS *Pegasus*? A dozen questions danced on her tongue, but she didn't think he'd answer a single one.

So she tried the squire when David Newton bespoke a moment of Sir Trevor's time to discuss the lack of an organ in the church.

"I am not familiar with the *Pegasus,* sir," she said, walking with the squire to where his carriage and the rest of his family were waiting. The squire boasted a fine son who was now a widower and attracting the attention of many of the young ladies in the village. The fact that he had an adorable baby daughter that sorely needed a mother was only icing on the cake.

"A fine twenty-eight-gun sixth-rate frigate," the squire said, rattling off terms that had no meaning to her. "Served under Nelson at one time. Grand gentleman. There will never be his like."

She remembered enough of her education at the vicarage school to know that the grand gentleman Admiral Horatio Nelson had died in 1805. Trevor certainly hadn't helped him sometime in 1811. Then who?

"A hero to be sure," she replied to the squire. "And I thank you for your kindness to Sir Trevor. A shame he couldn't join you."

His gaze drifted off across the churchyard to where the baronet stood listening politely while David Newton made his case. Even in the lacy shadows of the trees, the minister's face looked as red as his sister's. Apparently Sir Trevor was not in agreement about the need for more elaborate music.

"He'll find his place in Blackcliff," the squire mused. "I expect it will take some time. When a man isn't used to being welcomed, he may not recognize friendship when it's offered."

Gwen frowned at him, ready to ask what he meant, but the squire seemed to realize he might have said too much. He hurriedly excused himself and joined his family, lifting his granddaughter into his arms with a warm grin. All Gwen could do was return to Sir Trevor's side and puzzle over the matter.

Why would Sir Trevor not have been welcomed? He was handsome, he could be charming when he set his mind to it and he was certainly strong enough to do all the things Gwen thought a young gentleman might be expected to do: riding, boxing, hunting, fencing, dancing. He'd held some position of responsibility to have identified the administrative error and been awarded a baronetcy. Someone thought enough of him to purchase Blackcliff for him. He certainly seemed an honorable gentleman.

So, how could she make sure he felt welcome at Blackcliff?

Trevor was glad to return to the house. He did not like the disappointment in David Newton's eyes when Trevor had refused to purchase an organ for St. Martin's. It seemed the vicar had approached everyone of note in the congregation, and none had been willing to offer the funds. Trevor had been his last hope. Trevor had no idea whether music would improve the service at St. Martin's. He was just getting used to the idea of attending service at all. But he knew he had no funds to offer.

Gwen Allbridge had looked nearly as disappointed when he'd left her at the gatehouse. She'd gazed at him as if trying to picture him with two heads. Was she still wondering about his reaction to the squire? With any luck, she'd think it was merely because he intended to leave soon. He did not like to think of trying to fend off her questions. She would be a far more difficult adversary than David Newton.

He thought to spend the afternoon looking into the estate books in more depth, but his steward appeared at two, insisting that Trevor take up the ancient tradition of touring the boundary. Apparently the master of Blackcliff was expected to walk or ride along every edge of the estate on a regular basis, and a tour was long overdue.

Trevor hid his reluctance. Gwen had already pointed out that he could see every inch of his boundary from the top of Blackcliff Fell. As Rob Winslow and Horace Allbridge watched with obvious approval, Trevor mounted his horse and set off on the circuit his steward indicated.

Sitting on Icarus, trotting down the river bottoms with the hills rising all around him, the crisp autumn air streaming past, Trevor expected to feel the tug toward London. That was where his heart lay, after all. His entire life he'd worked to be accepted there, to be included among the aristocracy. With his baronetcy and an estate, he had never been closer to achieving his goal.

Instead, he had an overwhelming urge to gallop straight up the hill and launch Icarus into the sky as if they both might fly. He returned from his ride invigorated and relaxed, and Mrs. Bentley beamed at the way he attacked the venison she served him for dinner.

His thoughts were swiftly grounded the next day. Allbridge had finally located the surveyor's report, and Trevor read it eagerly as they sat in the library, a welcoming fire heating the dark room. Unfortunately, his steward was correct in his assessment. Colonel Umbrey had failed to make routine repairs on the mine, and now the timbers were sagging and the lower depths flooded. Without a significant investment, the Blackcliff Mine could not be reopened.

"Was he mad?" Trevor ranted, dropping the parchment onto the desk.

"Some thought so," Allbridge replied, lip out thoughtfully. "Claimed he was being hunted at the end. Locked himself in his room and refused to come out even to eat. Gwen found him dead one morning."

Trevor frowned. "Your daughter found him? What was she doing in the house?"

Allbridge shrugged. "Considers Blackcliff her home, Gwen does. You've seen it. Nothing happens in this house that she hasn't managed. She was one of the few the colonel trusted at the end, her and Mr. Newton."

Trevor could certainly understand why a man might want to lean on Gwen Allbridge. He'd never met anyone more determined or more capable. Every day she found something else to show him about his estate; just this morning she'd pulled him into the corridor to praise the magnificent oak paneling that covered every room in the Hall.

"You see how it's veined?" she had said, tracing the line with her hand, her dark eyes alight with appreciation. "And where each panel joins, a medallion." She'd grinned at him. "You won't find that in many houses."

He wouldn't find someone like Gwen Allbridge, either. He wanted to see the world through her eyes, where simple things like oak paneling and stone bridges were marvels. Yet he couldn't help wondering whether he'd end up like the previous master of Blackcliff—locked in his room, dying alone and raving. And he didn't relish the thought of explaining to the villagers that he wouldn't be reopening the mine, after all.

If his feelings toward Blackcliff weren't puzzling enough, there was the mystery of the little shepherd. Every time Trevor stepped out of the house for more than an hour, he'd return to find it missing from its station in the entryway. Once it had been located in the music room, another time in the dining room.

He'd gone so far as to ask Mrs. Bentley about it, but his housekeeper had turned as white as her hair and stared at Trevor so fixedly that he almost thought *he* was a ghost. After that, he caught her tiptoeing past the statue as she crossed the entryway.

Trevor was certain there had to be a logical explanation. Someone in the house seemed to think the statue belonged elsewhere. As it had moved before Mrs. Bentley, Rob Winslow and the maid, Dorie, had taken their posts, he could only wonder about his steward. Had Horace Allbridge been in the house the night Trevor had arrived? Was that why Gwen felt comfortable facing him with only an old pistol and the mastiff at her side? Yet Allbridge had had months with the empty house. He could have rearranged all the furnishings if he chose, and Trevor would never have been the wiser!

He was thinking about the puzzle again as he retired to bed his fourth night in Blackcliff. He was reaching for the handle on his bedchamber door when a flash of movement caught his eye. Hair rose along his arms as he turned. Dorie had already gone to bed. Rob Winslow slept over the stables. Mrs. Bentley had been in the butler's pantry; he'd called to her before retiring. No one else should be above stairs except Trevor.

Yet he swore that was a shadow disappearing down the stairs.

"You there!" he shouted, striding down the corridor. "Stop!"

He reached the stairs and pulled up short. The candles had been lit when he'd climbed to his room a few moments ago. Someone had snuffed them; he could smell the smoking wicks in the darkness. He could also just make out something moving below. Trevor threw himself after it.

"Stop, I say! Mrs. Bentley!"

With an audible crack, his foot collided with something solid, and Trevor pitched forward. He managed to pull in his arms and tuck his head, rolling with the momentum, but he felt the edges of the solid wood steps biting into his spine, his ribs. He fetched up on the landing with a grunt, and something thumped down beside him.

Trevor lay a hand over it, panting, even as he heard footsteps approaching and Mrs. Bentley's voice calling from below. A lamp flared.

He wasn't entirely surprised to find himself hugging the shepherd statue, chipped now from the collision. It seemed someone else besides Trevor thought it would make a good stumbling block for an enemy.

Chapter Nine

Though it was past time for bed, Gwen stood at the worktable in the gatehouse kitchen, fully dressed, gazing at her mother's recipe book. Her mother's precise handwriting marched down the stained page.

The horehound syrup was simple, just a few ingredients and instructions on how to steep them to bring out the flavors. Certainly it would be needed. All indications were that it would be a hard winter. But the syrup had been her mother's special recipe, the one cure everyone linked to her. How could Gwen be certain she'd do it justice? Besides, making the syrup without her mother felt wrong.

Someone pounded on the front door, the noise echoing through the little house. Gwen's heart started pounding, as well. Someone was sick. Knocks had come at all hours for her mother, who had been the village midwife and sometimes apothecary; now they came for her. It felt just as wrong, but she refused to think about anything except that she was needed. She gathered her skirts and hurried to answer the door even as her father clambered down the stairs, pulling on his coat as he came.

Rob Winslow stood on the step, face pale, eyes wide. "It's Sir Trevor. He fell."

Though she'd been ready for bad news, Gwen felt as if the floor had suddenly dipped. She snatched at Rob's arm and dug her fingers into the soft wool of his livery. "Is he alive?"

Rob nodded. "Aye, but in a great deal of pain. We need you."

"Go on," her father urged her. "I'll be right behind."

Her mind felt numb, but her mouth and her limbs seemed to know what to do. "Bring Mother's liniment and the cotton wrapping," Gwen told him, taking her wool cloak off the hook by the front door and throwing it about her shoulders. "And leave Dolly at home."

She was out the door with Rob before her father could nod agreement.

"What happened?" she asked as they hurried through the night. Rob's lantern cast a golden glow on the graveled drive, yet the grounds disappeared into darkness just beyond. Ahead, the entryway of Blackcliff Hall blazed like a beacon of hope.

"He fell down the stairs," Rob said, and she could hear the worry in his voice. "A strong man like him. How could such a thing happen?"

She knew a reason, but she hated even thinking that about Sir Trevor. Still, she had to know if she was to deal with his injuries. "Had he been drinking?"

"I don't think so. You'd have to ask Mrs. Bentley for sure, but I didn't smell anything when I checked him a moment before I left."

Gwen rounded on him. "Rob! You checked him and left him in pain? Why didn't you help him!"

"I only know horses," he protested, raising the lantern higher so she could see her way up the stairs to the door. "You know more about healing people, Miss Allbridge."

If only that were true. *Lord, help me to remember everything Mother taught me!*

Mrs. Bentley was fluttering about the entryway as Rob opened the door and let Gwen in.

"Oh, thank You, Lord!" she said as she took Gwen's hand and drew her close. "I couldn't move him by myself, and Rob ran off. I didn't know what to do."

"Allbridge!" Trevor's voice was a bellow from the landing, but it was the finest sound Gwen could have heard at that moment. She pulled off her cloak and ran to meet him.

He was sitting on the carpet of the landing, legs out in front of him, back up against the paneled wall as if he'd tried to use it to pull himself upright, and failed. Sweat stood on his brow, making his dark hair curl at the temples. Seeing Gwen, he raised his head and tried to smile. It was crooked.

"My father's on his way," she said, crouching beside him. "Rob says you fell."

"I tripped." He patted the shepherd statue, which was propped against the wall beside him. "This lad somehow found his way across the stairs."

Gwen frowned. She was certain the statue had been at its usual place in the entryway when she'd left that afternoon. It hadn't moved by itself.

Please, Lord, not another man lost to gin!

She leaned closer on the pretense of straightening the drape of his coat and took a surreptitious sniff. All she smelled was a hint of a musky cologne that reminded her of leather and old roses.

She glanced up to find him gazing at her with a gentle smile that made her feel unsteady. "I'm not drunk, Miss Allbridge."

"Certainly not," she said, straightening even as heat flushed up her.

Her father came through the door just then, and for the next few minutes, he and Rob worked at getting Sir Trevor on his feet without hurting him further. Gwen couldn't see them carrying him all the way to his bedchamber on the upper story, so she directed them down the last few stairs to the main floor and the music room just beyond.

"Gently," Gwen urged as they eased him onto the curved-back chaise longue. She'd thought the music room an odd place for the long couch when Colonel

Umbrey insisted it be moved from the upper sitting room after he'd had the Hall remodeled. The colonel had hardly been the type to sit and listen to anyone play the black enameled pianoforte in the corner of the room or the tall golden harp next to it. He'd never hosted musicales and filled the little rows of gilded, fan-backed chairs with guests. The fire Mrs. Bentley was lighting in the black marble fireplace was probably the first in years.

But Gwen was thankful now for the faded-green velvet chaise. It was probably the only piece of furniture on the main floor that would accommodate Sir Trevor's length.

"Move your fingers for me," she said as her father and Rob backed away from him and gave her room.

"My fingers aren't the problem," he assured her, but he held out his large hands and wiggled his fingers nonetheless.

Gwen refused to let him see her relief, though she sent up a prayer of thanks. As the village midwife, her mother had taught her any number of things about the way a human body reacted to sudden stress like a fall, illness or an impending birth.

"Now your toes," she insisted.

"You can't see them inside my boots," he pointed out, but his boots flexed as if he were obeying. His handsome face tightened in a grimace, and he sucked in a breath.

Gwen bent over his feet. "Which one?"

"Right," he grit out, body tensed.

Gwen could feel her father, Rob Winslow and Mrs. Bentley watching her. Rob had seen Gwen help his mother through pneumonia. Mrs. Bentley used Gwen's mother's liniment on her hands. Her father knew what she'd been trained to do. They all expected her to work a miracle.

You're the miracle worker, Lord. Help me.

Gently, she poised a hand on Trevor's right ankle, moved her fingers back and forth. It seemed beneath the supple leather she felt a hard lump that should not have been there.

"The boots have to come off," she told the others, straightening. "You'll probably have to cut the right one."

"No," Sir Trevor snapped, but she ignored him. It was hard enough to say the rest. She fixed her eyes on the middle button of Rob Winslow's brown coat.

"And I'll need you to remove his trousers, as well."

Bless Rob, but he didn't question her. "Aye, Miss Allbridge. I'll help the master."

"And Miss Allbridge and I will wait outside," Mrs. Bentley added as if to assure Sir Trevor of his privacy. "There's a lovely silk banyan that belonged to the colonel. We found it while cleaning. I'll just fetch it for you."

Gwen risked a glance at Sir Trevor. He nodded his thanks, but his face was pinched, as if he dreaded the jostling his leg was about to receive.

She gave him a commiserating smile before leaving him to Rob's good graces.

"Odd piece of business, that," her father said in the corridor as Mrs. Bentley hurried off after the banyan. "How'd that statue get in the middle of the stairs?"

Gwen held up a finger. "Don't you start, too! I heard Mrs. Bentley muttering about ghosts. You know there's no such thing."

"Oh, I've wondered. You don't think it strange, the colonel dying like he did?"

Gwen tried not to remember the day she'd found him white and cold. His eyes had been closed, but his hands had gripped the covers so tightly they'd had to cut the sheets to get him out of the bed. "He was an old man, Father. His heart gave out. The physician from Carlisle said so."

"Oh, aye. A fine fellow that physician was, too— let everyone know how put out he was to come all this way as a personal favor to the squire. I'd have felt a great deal better if you'd had a chance at the body."

"The coroner wouldn't have taken my word," Gwen reminded him. "I'm not even a midwife. Let us focus on the moment, if you please. I have little interest in discussing the previous master of Blackcliff when the current master needs us."

Mrs. Bentley returned down the corridor then, puffing from her exertions, a pale green silk banyan draped over her sturdy arms. She passed it in to

Rob, and, a few minutes later, he opened the door and let them all in.

Sir Trevor was leaning against the satin bolster Rob must have put at his back, his upper body and legs swathed in the elegant drape of the banyan. Rob had removed his cravat, as well, probably hoping to make him more comfortable, but Gwen could see the pulse beating at the base of his throat. She felt as if her own pulse was beating in time.

She forced herself to focus on his stockinged feet instead, where they protruded from the hem of the banyan. The ankle on the right was obviously the larger of the two.

"This may hurt," she warned him. As gently as she could, she probed the puffy flesh with her fingers, checking muscles, tendons, bone. A tremor ran up his long leg. She glanced at his face to find it white, his nostrils flared. But he said nothing, merely watching her, trusting her, eyes as green as the banyan.

Gwen straightened. "It doesn't seem to be broken, which is a blessing. I'd say you have a nasty sprain. You'll need to keep off it for a few days, perhaps a week."

He groaned, but she thought it was more from frustration than pain. "Impossible. I intended to ride for London by Friday."

Something tightened inside her. He was leaving? Had all her efforts come to naught? Had he found nothing worthwhile in Blackcliff, even her?

"I'm afraid that *is* impossible," she said. "Friday is only a few days away. Your ankle will never mend that fast, and I imagine you'll have a few other bruises that will protest a grueling ride, as well."

He shifted on the chaise as if feeling them even now. "There must be something you can do."

Oh, there were any number of things she could do, and she was ready to do nearly all of them to save Blackcliff. Gwen smiled at him. "I've some excellent liniment that should ease the pain."

As if on cue, her father stepped forward and handed her the clear jar with the peach-colored ointment inside. She'd rubbed it on many an elderly lady, yet she could not make herself open the jar. Instead, she held it lightly in her hand, staring at Sir Trevor's ankle.

Oh, but she didn't feel up to removing that sock, running her hands on his skin. And why had Mrs. Bentley stoked up that fire? The room must be sweltering.

She pushed the bottle at Rob. "You'll need to rub this in, morning and night."

He nodded. "I remember. Father swore it helped Ruby through last winter."

She could only hope he wouldn't tell Sir Trevor that Ruby was his father's favorite horse. "And cold compresses to reduce the swelling," she called to Mrs. Bentley, who was tidying up the little gilt chairs.

"Of course!" the housekeeper promised, hurrying to her side.

"That ought to help," Gwen told Sir Trevor, "but I cannot promise that you'll be ready to ride by Friday."

"With your determination," Sir Trevor said with a valiant smile, "I have no doubt I could fly by Friday if needed."

Her father clapped Rob on the shoulders. "We'll leave you to it, then, lad. Unless you need me, Sir Trevor."

Trevor's smile was slipping, and Gwen felt for him. "I'll be fine. Thank you for your care and concern."

Her father nodded, but Gwen hesitated to follow him out the door. She wanted to stay, to be the one to drape the cool cloths across Sir Trevor's ankle, to speak quietly and low to lull him to sleep, to keep watch over him that night in case he woke in pain.

But she knew it wasn't proper for her to stay. If people were already wondering whether she'd set her cap for him, they'd think she was out to trap him if she stayed the night in his company.

"I'll check on you in the morning," she promised before leaving the room.

Mrs. Bentley followed her out. "Now, don't you worry, dearie. I'll be sure to check on him tonight."

Gwen fought back the wave of envy those words brought. "Thank you, Mrs. Bentley. If he's in any kind of pain, try chamomile tea. My mother swore by it."

"I'll do that. And I think there's one of the colonel's canes in the umbrella stand by the kitchen door. I know you said Sir Trevor shouldn't be up and about, but I fancy he won't be one to stay abed."

Gwen was afraid the housekeeper was right. Sir Trevor had called her determined, but she'd never seen a man so fixed on leaving a place that welcomed him. The ache inside her only grew, and she feared it was for far more than the loss of Blackcliff Hall.

The housekeeper touched Gwen's arm, face turning serious. "And what about our positions, Miss Allbridge? If he leaves for London, will he want to keep a staff here?"

At least someone remembered the reason to keep Sir Trevor in the village. "I don't know," Gwen admitted, trying to block the worry from her voice.

Mrs. Bentley sighed. "I was so hoping to stay on here rather than spend the winter in the poorhouse in Evendale. I'm grateful for the kindness there, mind you, but it can be a dreary place."

So would the gatehouse be, Gwen was sure, once Sir Trevor rode away down the lane. But she couldn't think about that now or she very much feared she'd start crying.

"First we must heal him," she told Mrs. Bentley. "And we'll make life so simple and pleasant, he won't want to leave."

"So you've said," the housekeeper replied. "But he doesn't seem to find any pleasure in the place, and I don't see how this mishap will help."

Chapter Ten

Lying on the couch in the music room that night, watching the fire dying in the grate, Trevor thought he finally understood the nature of Blackcliff Hall. It was a giant maw that sucked in unwitting victims, chewed them thoroughly and spat them out in pieces. No matter that he'd tried to be a gentleman about leaving it behind. He could not escape now until his ankle healed. Someone, something, seemed determined to keep him here.

He'd have almost suspected Gwen Allbridge, except she was such a caring physician. Her hands on his ankle had been sure, her advice sound. And she was a far more comforting sight beside him than the best Edinburgh-trained physician in London.

"Where did she learn her skills?" he had asked Mrs. Bentley when his housekeeper had brought blankets and pillows to the music room to keep him comfortable on the chaise that night. He and Rob

Winslow had agreed that moving him for the time being was inadvisable.

"Miss Allbridge is likely to become the village midwife now that her lovely mother has passed on," Mrs. Bentley replied, gently draping a blanket over his injured leg and moving to pick up a pillow.

"A shame my foot wasn't about to give birth," he teased.

The housekeeper shoved the pillow behind him with considerably more force than he thought necessary. "Miss Allbridge and her mother nursed everything from a colicky colt to a crippled miner. There isn't a family in Blackcliff that hasn't a reason to wish her well."

"Yet she still finds time to help her father manage the estate," he marveled.

"Gwendolyn Allbridge is what keeps Blackcliff together, sir." She pulled back and eyed Trevor sternly. "We should all be thankful she's so giving." Her smile was forced. "And will you want anything else this night?"

Trevor had the feeling that he wasn't going to get it even if he asked. Instead, he thanked the housekeeper and sent her on her way, then settled back on the chaise.

It was a difficult night. First he found it hard to relax, remembering how he'd come to this pass. Had it been only a shadow on the stair, perhaps from one of the suits of armor? Then why had the statue been waiting for him? Had there been someone in the house who had fled to avoid capture, or had that someone been trying to lure Trevor into a trap? At least all the activity in the house had likely scared off the perpetrator.

He also found rest a long ways off because of his body. Gwen had been right—his spine, his rear end and one shoulder ached from his roll down the stairs, and his ankle throbbed. Though Rob Winslow helped him shave the next morning, Trevor knew he must look the worse for wear. His right boot was a loss; he could only hope the village of Blackcliff boasted a cobbler who could make him a new pair. Perhaps if Trevor sold some of the chairs in this room, he could pay for them.

He made himself eat the excellent breakfast his housekeeper served him only because she stood there watching him the entire time. After he swallowed the last bite of the poached eggs and bacon, he thanked her for her trouble and sent her about her duties.

But the quiet of the music room quickly bored him. The room was dimly lit by a few candles in sconces along the far wall. Situated as he was, he couldn't have reached any of the portfolios of music if he tried, and he wasn't sure what he would have done with them had he succeeded.

It was warm enough with the newly made fire, but with the curtains drawn there was little to relieve his mind of his aches, either physical or financial. When Gwen poked her head in the room later that morning, he must have looked as desperate as he felt, for she rushed to his side.

"Are you in pain?" she cried, depositing the bundle she'd been carrying on the carpet with a thud. "I left instructions to give you chamomile."

Before he knew what she intended, she'd rested her hand on his forehead, as if checking for fever. The cool touch sent a jolt through him, and he leaned back from it. "I'm fine, Miss Allbridge. I don't need medicine like some invalid."

She rolled her eyes as she drew back her hand. "There's no shame in taking medicine when it's needed."

"I didn't need it," he insisted.

She tsked and bent to look at his ankle. He felt his muscles tensing, preparing for the pain when she touched it and forced them to relax. But her fingers were gentle.

"The swelling is going down already, thank God," she reported. "But you won't be on your feet for a few days."

This time Trevor did groan.

"I know this isn't easy for you," she said as she straightened. She drew up one of the little gilt chairs and seated herself beside him. "You are clearly a man of action. So, I brought you a few things to pass the time." She picked up her bundle and set it on her lap.

Why did he feel like a child on Christmas morn,

hoping for a present on the table? He had long out-grown such childish hopes.

There was a decided twinkle in her dark eyes as she pulled a long brass tube from her bundle.

"A spy glass?" Trevor eyed it with interest.

"We'll open the drapes," she promised as she handed it to him. "From here you should be able to see halfway up Blackcliff Fell. You wait—I imag-ine you'll find a veritable parade. Deer, birds, rabbit, perhaps even a fox."

"How delightful," he drawled.

Gwen shook her head. She was wearing a simple cotton frock of a dark russet, patterned in cream flowers. The color brought out the fire in her hair; the drape, just under her bosom, emphasized the curve of her figure.

"Don't think you can win the prize for worst pa-tient," she scolded him. "Colonel Umbrey bore that distinction."

Trevor snorted. "Small wonder, stuck in this house."

"Oh, yes, stuck in a warm, sound home with good food and people at your beck and call. Such a dif-ficult life, I'm sure."

It was not the place but the time that concerned him. "I've had worse."

"Really?" She looked utterly unconvinced, but he was not about to explain his odd upbringing. "Well," she continued, "perhaps this will take your mind off it." She pulled out a large book, with a crimson leather binding and gilded lettering along the spine.

Trevor took it eagerly, then sagged when he saw the title. "The Bible?"

She frowned. "Certainly the Bible. What better comfort can there be?"

A fortune in gold? His birthright acknowledged? A real estate within a day's ride of London? Any of those would have eased the pain inside him more than this heavy tome.

"I suppose it would be useful to prop up my ankle," he said, trying to find something kind to say.

She seized the book and pulled it back onto her lap. "You know, sometimes I'm not sure when you're teasing me. But I'll tell you what. You lean back, and I'll read to you. What's your favorite passage?"

Did he have a favorite? Did he even know a passage to recommend to her? His mother had few books at her house, and he was certain none of them had been a Bible.

He leaned back and closed his eyes. "You choose something."

"The whole point is to comfort you, sir," she said, rather primly, he thought. "What stories did your mother read you as a child?"

"The scandal sheets," he said before he thought better of it.

"The scandal sheets?" Instead of shocked, she sounded genuinely puzzled. He opened his eyes, trying to think of a way to explain the cheap papers carrying gossip about the finest families to those who could barely afford the penny price to read them.

But her brow was clearing. "Oh, of course. First and Second Samuel are rather scandalous."

Was that a blush on her cheeks? In a moment, she'd be as red as Ruth Newton. What exactly was in that book? "What did your mother read you?" he asked, curious.

She smoothed her hand over the fine leather. "She was partial to the Psalms, especially the happy ones. She was that kind of person—happy, busy, full of joy and life. She loved everyone around her, and they knew it."

"You are much like her, I think," he murmured.

"Oh, I hope so." He heard the tremor in her voice.

Remembering clearly hurt, yet he envied her. What must it be like to be raised by a mother who sincerely cared? Who was admired for the good she did rather than the body she offered to those who paid well?

"I am sorry for your loss," he said. "Has she been gone long?"

"Just over a year." She sucked in a breath as if trying to steady herself. "Forgive me, Sir Trevor. I seem to be a watering pot this morning. And I came here to cheer you. What about the story of David and Goliath? A rousing adventure ought to suit you."

He'd listen to the entire book if doing so would

bring back the smile to her face. "That would be greatly appreciated."

She nodded, smile returning though still a little strained. "It's not the scandal sheets, I fear, but I'm not up to reading them today." Blush returning, she bowed her head over the book and rustled the gilt-edged pages as she sought her place.

Trevor rested his head on the pillow and listened to her clear, warm voice read the story. The words were a little old-fashioned and formal, but Gwen's animation made the pictures come alive in his mind. And though he quite enjoyed the story of young David besting the mighty warrior, he couldn't wait to get his hands on that book and find out just what Gwen Allbridge considered scandalous enough to blush over.

Her plan was working. Gwen could feel it. Despite the pain in his ankle, Sir Trevor was smiling more, and more genuinely. She had caught no sign of his polite face. Mrs. Bentley reported that he ate better, too.

Whenever Gwen visited, and she made a point of visiting frequently, he regaled her with stories about the creatures he'd seen out the window, the stories he'd read in the Bible. Blackcliff was finally weaving its spell over him, and she had every hope he would succumb to it.

Nevertheless, over the next three days, she kept up her campaign to win him over. She had the best cooks in the village send up delicacies for his table. She invited Mrs. Petersham, an accomplished pianist, to come play for him, and Mr. Thornton, who had a fine baritone voice, to come sing. Mr. Eastley the cobbler came to measure him for a new pair of boots and clucked over the state of his ankle.

She scoured the library for other interesting books he might like to read. She allowed her father to visit only when he could offer some new reason to praise the estate or enlist Sir Trevor's aid to solve some minor problem.

She was a little worried about leaving her father to his own devices, but he moved about the Hall with surety as if knowing what needed to be done and taking pride in doing it. She sent up a prayer that his work would keep him too busy to go looking for other solace.

She managed to locate Colonel Umbrey's ivory-and-ebony chess set in a cupboard in the schoolroom, but she knew she wasn't the person to challenge Sir Trevor. Instead, she dragged David Newton to the Hall to play. Ruth accompanied her brother, and Gwen helped Mrs. Bentley by laying out the tea things for the group on one of the tables Rob Winslow had been persuaded to carry to the music room.

"I'm glad you came, Newton," Sir Trevor said after he'd beaten the minister in remarkably few moves. He was still confined to the chaise longue, but Gwen was hoping he might be able to move about the lower floors by the next day.

The room had become more comfortable but definitely more crowded. Two leather-bound chairs from the library stood next to the chaise to allow visitors to converse easily with him. A decorative table inlaid with teak flanked him on either side to hold his entertainments, and a lap desk rested on the floor where he could lift it when he wished to review or compose correspondence.

David and Ruth had dressed their best for the visit. The minister was in his Sunday suit, all black with a pristine white cravat and somber gray-striped waistcoat. Gwen was determined to ask Ruth about the pattern for the dusky-green wool gown she wore with its puffed upper sleeves and graceful hem. It quite put Gwen's cotton gown in the shade. Ruth's blush had yet to fade from Sir Trevor's praise as she'd entered.

"I've been wanting to ask you a few questions about the Bible," Trevor said to the minister now as Gwen poured tea and handed it around.

David Newton raised a brow. "Oh?" He glanced at Gwen and Ruth as if hoping they might melt away. "Well, I suppose I can be of some help. What exactly is troubling you?"

"The amount of violence, terror and mayhem," Sir Trevor replied with a slight frown.

"Oh!" Ruth cried, one hand going to her mouth and saucer shaking in the other.

Sir Trevor inclined his head toward her. "Forgive my plain speaking, Miss Newton, but that is exactly my point. One does not expect such things from the Holy Word. Yet it's filled with stories about ordinary people doing extraordinary things. Saving the world's animals from a flood, escaping some Egyptian king right through the sea, fighting off giants."

He made it sound as if all these were new to him. Gwen frowned in surprise, but David Newton smiled.

"Ah, the Old Testament," the minister mused. "Yes, I imagine it does seem a little tumultuous if you've had a steady diet of the epistles. But you'll find the Old and New Testaments go hand in glove when you've looked a little deeper."

Sir Trevor nodded thoughtfully, then held out his plate to Gwen. "Might I trouble you for another of Miss Newton's excellent buns, Miss Allbridge? Your friend is truly gifted."

She was happy to oblige, though Ruth flushed beet and stammered her thanks. But Gwen noticed Sir Trevor was far quieter after that, and it wasn't long before the Newtons made their excuses and rose to leave.

"An interesting gentleman," Ruth murmured to Gwen as Gwen walked with her to the door. "He seems to be settling in."

Gwen squeezed her arm. "I think so, too."

Ruth's look softened. "And you enjoy his company, I think. Be careful, dearest. He's said nothing about making Blackcliff his seat, has he?"

"No," Gwen admitted. "But he will. How could he do otherwise with all the fine company we've given him?"

Ruth's honey-colored brows gathered. "Very easily, I imagine. We are what some might call rustic. A gentleman like him may not appreciate that." She flushed red again. "Forgive me. I just don't want to see you disappointed."

But Gwen was certain disappointment was less of a possibility every day. As soon as Ruth and David were on their way, she hurried back to Sir Trevor's side.

He brightened at the sight of her, and she swore the room brightened, as well. "You are kind to bring me so many diversions," he said as she gathered up the tea things. "Yet I cannot help but wonder whether I offended the Newtons just now."

"Doubtful," she assured him. "I'm sure Mr. Newton is pleased to share what he knows." She refused to mention how Ruth had a hard time keeping her gaze away from Sir Trevor for very long. Gwen had a feeling he had the same effect on most unmarried ladies.

He sighed. "I feel as if I'm learning things for the first time."

Gwen perched on the chair Ruth had just vacated. "Isn't that amazing? You can read the stories and reread the stories in the Bible, and each time, you learn something new."

"You see that, too?" He sounded pleased. "It truly is a remarkable book. And you, Miss Allbridge, are a remarkable woman. You see to my every need, before I know the need is even there."

Gwen grinned at him. "It has been my pleasure, sir, I assure you."

He eyed her a moment, head tilted as if he was thinking. "I wonder, would you do me the honor of calling you by your first name?"

Pleasure rippled through her, and her heart started beating faster. "I'd be delighted, Sir Trevor."

"Trevor, please." He ran his finger over the binding of the Bible as it sat on the table beside him. "And I must thank you for this. It turned out much better than I'd expected."

She could only hope he felt the same way about the rest of Blackcliff. "I know," she teased. "I've yet to see you use it to prop up your foot."

But she also knew he'd need more to keep himself busy as his ankle started to heal. Trevor needed something to take his mind off London, to help him become the true master of Blackcliff. And she knew just the thing.

Chapter Eleven

Trevor was making his way through Psalms when Gwen appeared in the doorway of the withdrawing room the next day. She'd handed him an ebony-handled cane and his new boots the previous afternoon and helped him hobble out of the music room for the first time in days. Even the cooler air in the corridor smelled fresher to Trevor, but the walk down it and up the stairs to his bedchamber had set his ankle to throbbing, and he'd had to rest it on an embroidered footstool this morning after making the trek back down again.

Now, despite how fetching Gwen looked in her pale sprigged muslin gown, he found himself reluctant to put the Bible down. Gwen had said her mother favored the Psalms because they were happy, but it seemed to him that the psalmist had complained to God about any number of things—sickness, poverty, enemies in pursuit, evildoers triumphing. Every psalm ended in praise for God's mercy, His faithfulness and His love. Did God really listen to the fears and concerns of humans? Would He listen to someone like Trevor?

"Good morning, Sir Trevor," Gwen announced. She was back to using his title, which alerted him that something was up. He smiled politely and set the Bible aside.

"Good morning, Gwen." Saying her name felt right, and he knew his smile was broadening. "And what can I do for you this morning?"

She stepped aside to allow his housekeeper to enter the withdrawing room. Mrs. Bentley blinked and took hesitant steps, dark skirts swishing against the carpet. She glanced around as if expecting someone to come leaping over the chairs at her.

"Mrs. Bentley is ready for her interview," Gwen explained.

He did not like to appear dense, but he could not think what she meant. He'd already questioned his housekeeper about the statue lying across the stairs. Mrs. Bentley had promised she'd seen no one and heard nothing out of the ordinary until Trevor had called for help.

"Interview?" he asked. "What interview?"

"For her position as housekeeper." Gwen's smile was overbright. "I know you haven't had an opportunity to settle on your staff, so I arranged the interviews for today."

Mrs. Bentley shoved her plump hands into the

pockets of her crisp white apron and stoically regarded the carpet.

Much as Trevor admired Gwen Allbridge's energy and determination, there were moments when she came dangerously close to overstepping her bounds. He hadn't settled on a staff because he didn't want a staff.

While he'd been stuck in the music room, he'd tried to determine how he might take care of the ones who were serving him at the moment. Honor demanded that he not allow them to go unpaid.

If he sold the silver tea service, he might have enough to pay Mrs. Bentley, Rob Winslow and Dorie. He hoped they would find work elsewhere, with a good character recommendation. He might have enough left over to pay Horace Allbridge for his work thus far, but Trevor hadn't figured out how to keep paying the man for maintaining the estate in Trevor's absence.

He certainly had no intention of hiring anyone else on a permanent basis. But he had avoided explaining that to the good people of Blackcliff because they seemed to see the master of Blackcliff as some sort of god. After reading the Bible these past few days, he had to own it all seemed a bit blasphemous.

So he stood as a gentleman should do in the presence of a lady, leaning on his cane with one hand and motioning to his housekeeper with the other.

"Certainly, Mrs. Bentley. If you would have a seat, we can discuss your qualifications for this post."

The woman blanched but ventured closer, pausing to take her hands out of her pockets and adjust a lamp on the side table. She sank onto a nearby chair and bunched her hands in her lap. "Qualifications, sir?"

"I'm sure Sir Trevor already knows what a good cook and housekeeper you are," Gwen assured her, hovering near the doorway. She cast him a glance that said she hoped he wouldn't upset the little housekeeper.

Trevor nodded to Gwen. "I certainly do. Thank you for bringing her to my attention, Miss Allbridge. We'll let you know as soon as we're finished here."

Gwen stiffened. "Oh, of course. I'll just be in the library with Father if anyone needs me." With a last look of puzzlement to Trevor, as if she couldn't understand his mood, she disappeared down the corridor.

"I am very grateful for this position, sir," Mrs. Bentley said as soon as Trevor turned his gaze to her. The housekeeper must have tidied up before coming into the room, for every white strand was neatly tucked into her coronet braid and even the collar on her black bombazine gown stood at attention. "If you should see your way clear to hire me permanently, I'll do my best to give good service."

Her hands continued to worry in the white apron.

Did this post mean so much to her, then? "Why do you want to be Blackcliff's housekeeper?" he asked.

Her eyes widened. "It's a good house, Sir Trevor, a fine house. I'd be honored to serve it."

He suspected half the village would say the same. "What did you do before you worked at Blackcliff?"

Her round face sagged. "I kept house for my family. But they're all gone now, sir."

Her voice had turned hollow. "Have you no other relatives elsewhere?" Trevor asked with a frown. "No one you'd care to stay with?"

"My husband and children are buried in St. Martin's churchyard. So are my mother and father and all my sisters and brothers and their children. Where else would I go?"

So, like Gwen Allbridge, Margaret Bentley's world was Blackcliff. Was that one of the reasons he longed to return to London? Was he afraid of the world shrinking to this tiny village? Would that be so very bad?

Once, even a few days ago, he would have answered a resounding yes. Now, he wasn't so sure. Blackcliff had much to recommend it, just as Gwen had said. Here, he was master of all he surveyed, respected. But would they all be so respectful if they knew he could not afford to keep up this life? He could not maintain Blackcliff if he couldn't lay his hands on some ready cash and soon.

"Will you stay, Sir Trevor?" she asked, as if reading his thoughts. "I know you won't have need of a housekeeper if you decide to close up the house."

She was right, of course. He'd already determined she would be one of the people he'd have to let go. Yet how difficult would it be to allow her to stay in her room over the kitchen? They appeared to have plenty of fuel laid up; Gwen Allbridge wouldn't let her starve. And she clearly had nowhere else to go.

"And what would Blackcliff Hall be without a housekeeper to keep her?" he replied. "And as long as this estate is mine, Mrs. Bentley, you are welcome to stay."

"Oh!" Tears pooled in her eyes, and her lower lip quivered. "Oh, thank you, sir, and God bless you!"

She looked for a moment as if she'd launch herself at him. Trevor held up a hand. "I should be the one to thank you. Never have I been so well fed and cared for. You are a credit to your position."

Now her round cheeks were turning pink. "Thank you, sir." She rose unsteadily to her feet. "Shall I tell Miss Allbridge you're ready for the next interview?"

Oh, no, there were more? He could only hope the others had less touching stories to tell. "Very well, but I do have one question for you. Why are you moving that shepherd statue?"

It was a gambit. He could see no reason why his housekeeper would move the thing about. She hadn't the temperament to want to provoke the master.

She clutched her apron to her chest. "As God

is my witness, sir, I have done no more than put it back." She peered at him. "You haven't perhaps moved him, as a little joke?"

Trevor would have liked nothing better than to put her mind at ease. "Not I. Perhaps Dorie."

She visibly swallowed. "No, sir. I asked her especially. And neither have Mr. Allbridge or Miss Allbridge or Rob Winslow. It frightens me."

"Have you seen anyone else about on the other days?" Trevor pressed. "In the house or on the grounds?"

She shook her head. "No, sir. But then I'm a little isolated in the kitchen. If I hadn't been in the pantry the night you fell, I might not have found you until daybreak."

The thought gave him no comfort. If she hadn't come at his shout, would his mysterious enemy have returned for him? Trevor had seen no sign of further disturbances, but then his vista had been limited.

And why had Mrs. Bentley been in the butler's pantry so late at night? He'd only called to her initially before heading to bed because he hadn't seen her. Yet he could not suspect her of anything nefarious. Her face was too open, and she seemed genuinely concerned about that roaming statue. He thanked her again and sent her off to notify Gwen.

The next one to arrive for an interview was Rob Winslow, but Trevor set him talking about horses, and the two parted with no promises made. Dorie followed, but she kept blinking her great big eyes at him like an owl facing the morning, and the best he could do was send her from the room before she burst into tears.

The final interview was for the position of his valet, or so Gwen announced when she ushered in an elderly man. He had silvery hair pomaded back from a long face; his clothes, though behind the times, were neat and well made. His gray eyes were sharp as steel as he gazed at Sir Trevor, and his pride was evident in the way he walked into the room, head up, pace measured. He looked familiar, but Trevor couldn't place him.

"Sir Trevor, this is Mr. John Cord," Gwen said. Though she'd been hanging about the house all afternoon, she still looked as fresh as when Trevor had first seen her earlier. "He was valet to the previous master of Blackcliff." She smiled at the fellow encouragingly, then grinned at Trevor. "I thought you would appreciate a man of his experience."

Certainly he would, had he been able to afford one. Only his closest friends knew he employed no valet. They joked that he was too fussy or too determined to keep his privacy, and he encouraged the illusion. Better they thought him high in the instep than to know that his pockets were empty. He'd even had to write to a friend to send Trevor more of his clothes now that he had to stay longer than he'd intended at Blackcliff. The trunk had arrived the other day by the mail coach.

Cord coughed discretely into a handkerchief and

tucked the cloth up his sleeve with a flourish. "A pleasure to meet you, Sir Trevor."

To Trevor's surprise, Gwen's smile faded, and she took the fellow's elbow and led him to the closest chair.

"I'll be right back with tea," she promised. Her look to Trevor over the shoulder of the valet's gray coat was tight with worry. What had she seen that Trevor had missed?

He started the interview the same way he had the others, by asking Cord why he wanted to be a valet at Blackcliff. But Cord didn't talk about family or the difficulty in finding other work. He grimaced, glanced toward the doorway as if to make sure Gwen was out of earshot, then leaned forward.

"In truth, Sir Trevor, I came today as a favor to Miss Allbridge. I've known her since she was a child. She's like a daughter to me. I find it hard to resist her entreaties."

Trevor knew the feeling. "Miss Allbridge's cheery determination is a welcome part of Blackcliff."

The valet nodded. "I didn't want to disappoint her, but I have little interest in taking up my old post."

Trevor raised a brow. "And why not? You seem to have a few more years in you."

Cord smiled grimly. "Perhaps not as many as you might think. But I'd work in that damp dark mine of yours before I'd consent to live in this house again."

He paused to cough into his fist, gaze flickering up to Trevor's, then down again. He was clearly giving Trevor time to think about that statement.

"I imagine some might not like returning to the house where their last master met his end," Trevor said, feeling his way.

"Oh, it's not that, sir," he said, lowering his hand. "Blackcliff Hall is cursed, has been for generations."

Cursed? What nonsense was this? His skepticism must have shown on his face, for Cord narrowed his eyes.

"Haven't you seen it? Strange people appearing and disappearing. Furniture and knickknacks moving about by themselves. This house isn't healthy." He shivered and coughed again as if to prove it.

Though Trevor had seen the very things the fellow described, he couldn't believe they were caused by some curse. Before he could say as much, Gwen hurried back in, carrying a bundle of cloth in her arms.

"The kettle's on the boil," she said, moving to their sides. "But it can be chilly in here. I thought you might want this."

Trevor thought she meant to tuck another blanket around him, and he held up his hand to fend her off. But she went behind the valet instead, shaking out a dark wool cloak the fellow must have brought with him and draping the material around his slender shoulders. It settled about him like smoke, cloaking even his face for a moment.

Recognition was instant. Trevor knew that cloak, he knew the gloved hand that extended from it. Cord had been the man who'd taken Icarus from him the night he'd arrived.

The only question was what Trevor intended to do about it.

Chapter Twelve

Gwen saw the change in Trevor. It was very much like watching Dolly wake to a strange sound. His body stiffened, his head came up and his eyes narrowed. Goodness, what troubled him? Was it that she'd looked after Mr. Cord's needs before his?

"Forgive me, Sir Trevor," she said as soothingly as she could. "I should have thought to ask. Are you warm enough?"

Calculation flickered in those jade eyes, and she nearly groaned aloud. She'd just given him an excellent excuse to send her from the room, and she was certain he'd take it. She'd fully intended to participate in the interviews, to ease them along. Not that Trevor was incapable of choosing his own staff; she just wanted to help.

But, with the exception of Mrs. Bentley, who'd come beaming from the room to throw her arms about Gwen in thanks, none of the others had been able to assure Gwen they'd been given a position. Trevor hadn't refused anyone, exactly, but neither had he given them reason to hope.

She'd thought surely it would be different with John Cord. Unlike the others, he had years of experience. Besides, he badly needed to work. Unfortunately, from what she'd just seen, he was in far worse trouble.

"I am a bit chilled," Trevor replied. "I believe there's an exceptional wool blanket in the upstairs sitting room. Perhaps you'd be so kind as to bring it down."

Oh, but he was a canny one. He knew the trek would take her several minutes at best. He was going to pounce on poor Mr. Cord, and he didn't want her here to witness it.

"Certainly," Gwen said cheerfully. "But I'll just stoke up the fire first. You two go right ahead. Don't mind me."

She turned her back on him, pretending not to notice the shake of his dark head. Her steps to the hearth were slow and measured, her ears straining.

"Had you other questions for me, Sir Trevor?" Mr. Cord asked, with charming grace, Gwen thought.

She picked up the brass poker and opened the iron door on the stove inset in the fireplace. Heat bathed her.

"Have you always been a valet?" Trevor asked. "For some reason, I see you handling horses."

The poker slid from Gwen's fingers and clattered on the stone hearth even as Mr. Cord began coughing. He'd been the man to take Icarus? She knew he was given to walking on the estate from time to time. She and Dolly had come across him once, and he'd told her as much.

"It reminds me of happier times," he'd said in that slow, mournful voice of his, and, of course, she'd assured him it was quite all right. But she'd never dreamed he'd be so familiar as to take a horse from a gentleman he'd never met or agreed to serve!

"Water," he croaked now, and Gwen raised her skirts to kick shut the door, then hurried back to the table. Though there was a glass and a pitcher sitting in easy reach, Trevor made no move to help the valet. Gwen poured a glass and held it out to Mr. Cord. She frowned at Trevor, but his gaze was narrowed on the valet.

"Forgive me," Mr. Cord said at last, handing the glass back to Gwen. "I don't know much about horses, but I thought I could at least be of service when you rode up that night." He lowered his gaze to his gloved hands, which had tightened into fists in his lap. "It's been a long time since I could be of service."

Gwen hurt for him. "There, now," she said, setting the glass on the table. "Sometimes we are called to serve, and sometimes others are called to serve us. Come back to the kitchen when you're finished here. I'm sure Mrs. Bentley has something to spare."

He stood and drew the cloak around him as if it were his pride. "No need for charity, Miss Allbridge. I've always been able to take care of myself." He bowed his head to Trevor. "If you have no other questions, sir?"

Trevor's eyes remained narrowed as he looked up at the fellow. "What do you know of a shepherd statue?"

Mr. Cord coughed into his fist before answering. "The Shepherd of Nice? Colonel Umbrey purchased it in France, I believe, during a time when we weren't at war. He was inordinately fond of the piece and moved it from room to room so he could always keep it in view."

Gwen felt as if the breath of winter had blown down the corridor. No! She did not believe in ghosts! But could someone else be moving the statue in the colonel's memory? The only one besides John Cord who had served him was her father.

"Thank you," Trevor said, leaning on his cane to stand. "If I have further questions, I'll let you know."

Cord nodded. "I hope you'll consider what I said, Sir Trevor. Blackcliff Hall can be an unforgiving place. Good day."

Gwen could only watch as he made his way to the door, cough trailing in his wake.

"Something isn't right," Trevor said, watching him, as well.

Gwen quite agreed. "You could have been kinder,"

she said, gathering up the glass and pitcher. "He's obviously unwell."

"Exactly what I want in a valet," he quipped.

Gwen made a face. "Well, I didn't know that before I sent word to him about the interview." She hugged the pitcher close. She should help John Cord, but she feared she knew what would do the most good. "I'll see if Mrs. Wheaton has any of the horehound syrup to spare. It's proven helpful for consumption."

Trevor frowned. "Consumption? That's a leap from a cough, isn't it?"

"A cough, blood on his handkerchief, wasting away. Mother always said those were telltale signs." Gwen felt hollow, remembering. "She had them all in the end."

"Forgive me," he said, and his voice had lost that cutting quality that sometimes infused it. "Of course you would recognize the symptoms."

She sighed. "Only too well. And, of course, you'd recognize the man who took Icarus. For what it's worth, I don't think he meant any harm."

"No," he agreed, eyes narrowing once more, "but someone does. He said the house was cursed."

She was surprised how easily the laugh bubbled up. "That's ridiculous. There's nothing wrong with Blackcliff that a little hard work won't fix."

"And you've noticed nothing odd about the place?"

"Not since you arrived. Before then, we had some trouble with vagrants."

"Ah, yes, so you said. Could one or more of them have stayed on, perhaps hidden in the house?"

The room was only getting colder. She set down the glass and pitcher and marched back to the fire to lay on more coal. "Certainly not," she said as she worked. "I told you—we scrubbed from the schoolroom to the laundry."

"But not the cellar," he reminded her.

Why couldn't she get warm? "I see why you wanted that blanket," she said. "It's unreasonably cold in here." She watched the flames turn blue. "There. That's better."

"Someone is moving that shepherd statue," he said quietly. "I won't believe it moves on its own. And I don't believe in ghosts."

"Neither do I," she said, turning to face him. Their gazes met, his thoughtful. He offered her a smile, and the room was finally warm.

"That statue stood in the middle of this room the night we met," Gwen said. "I didn't move it, and neither did you. So you're right—someone else was in the house that night."

"Besides Dolly?"

He was teasing her, all charm, yet she thought she knew why. He must have seen he was frightening her and was trying to make light of it. But the thought of someone hiding in the house, watching them, unnerved her.

"Definitely besides Dolly," she said, returning to his side. "But it strikes me that Dolly may be the solution to the problem. She doesn't like strangers. Perhaps we should give her the run of the house, see if she notices anything."

"Excellent idea." He fingered the cane as if eager for a fight. "When can we start?"

Gwen picked up the glass and pitcher once more and started for the door. "I'll ask Father to bring her up as soon as the last interview is over."

"Gwen." The sound of her given name as well as the gentle tone, soft as a caress, pulled her up short. She glanced back to find him regarding her sadly.

"That was the last interview," he said. When she opened her mouth to protest, he held up one hand. "I appreciate your help, but I have no need to hire a staff. As soon as I can settle things to my liking, I mean to return to London."

She wanted to scream, to throw the glass in her hand against the wall, to rail at the ceiling. She would never be as perfect as her mother, but she couldn't have failed. She'd worked so hard!

"Why?" she asked. "I thought you were coming to enjoy Blackcliff."

He shifted on his feet, but she didn't think it was his ankle that pained him. "I have come to appreciate Blackcliff in many ways. I simply need to return to London."

A man like him must journey to the capital from

time to time, she supposed. Hadn't the squire said as much?

She took a step closer, fingers tightening on the glass. "But you'll return, perhaps in the spring."

"The Season starts in the spring."

And, of course, he couldn't miss that. She knew about the Season, the months between Easter and the summer recess of Parliament. Men went up to make laws; women went up to find husbands. She was certain any number of ladies would be watching for his return. Perhaps the next time she saw him he'd be married to one. The thought only depressed her spirits further.

"You need have no concerns," he said as if he could see her distress. "I plan to close up the house, but Mrs. Bentley will stay on over the kitchen. You and your father are welcome to stay in the gatehouse. If you and Dolly keep an eye on the place, I'll consider it a fair trade for rent."

His offer was more than fair; it was generous. Yet it wasn't what she wanted. She wanted her father working, Blackcliff renovated, the village rescued. She wanted things to run the way they always had, before her mother and Colonel Umbrey had passed on. And, like John Cord, she hated living on charity.

"I'll just go tell Mrs. Bentley there will be no call for tea," she murmured. "And I'll send word you're through with interviews. I won't mention yet you're leaving. Father and I can let the village know about that and the mine after you've gone."

"I won't leave you to bear their discontent," he said. "I'll make the announcement before I go."

Thoughtful to the end. Gwen felt a tear forming and purposefully turned away from him. "As you wish."

But none of this was as she wished.

Trevor watched Gwen walk out the door. Her shoulders were slumped, her head turned away from him. He felt as if he'd snuffed out the last candle in the house. He tried to tell himself it was better this way—she should know the truth, and sooner rather than later. But the truth did not seem so noble when it brought her such pain.

As for John Cord, Trevor could not help but wonder whether he had been the shadow disappearing down the stairs the night Trevor had tripped. Yet how could the valet get into the house unseen? And that cough would surely give him away.

No, someone else must wish for Trevor to leave Blackcliff. Even though Trevor knew he was about to make that wish come true, he could not rest until he'd uncovered the mystery. Doing otherwise felt too much like leaving Gwen in danger.

True to her word, she brought Dolly back with her a short time later. The mastiff seemed to have caught her mistress's melancholy, for she whined and tugged at her leash as Gwen led her into the withdrawing room. He thought surely she'd knock Gwen off her feet, but Gwen ordered the dog down and Dolly lay obediently, if with accusing eyes, on the floor next to Trevor's chair.

"I've been thinking about what you said," Gwen told him, taking a seat next to him. Her hand reached out and stroked Dolly's massive head. "Everyone in the village will be heartbroken you're leaving."

That he very much doubted. At the very least David Newton would heave a sigh of relief that Trevor no longer plagued him with odd questions. "I think you give Blackcliff Hall too much importance," he replied as gently as he could.

Her hand stayed a moment, then continued its rhythmic motion. Dolly's head slowly drooped to the carpet and out of Gwen's reach.

"And you make too little of it," Gwen said in as kind a tone. "Is there nothing I can do to encourage you to stay?"

She could not know she was the one reason he hesitated. What man would be immune to her beauty, her energy, her compassion? Yet he could not offer her a place in his life. He could not afford to marry Gwen Allbridge any more than he could afford to keep Blackcliff. "There's nothing to be done, not unless you have a few hundred pounds of sterling stashed away."

He meant it as a joke, but her head came up as if

she'd caught the scent. "But you're a baronet. Surely you have funds at your disposal."

He should lie. He'd always lied, evaded or otherwise turned the conversation when it came to money. "Oddly enough, the Crown does not see fit to pass out guineas with titles," he joked, and he was rather pleased by the lack of bitterness in the statement.

"But Icarus, your belongings," she protested. She cocked her head and eyed him. "You do not look impoverished, Trevor."

And that was to his credit. She had no idea how hard it was to maintain the facade some days. Icarus he had won in a wager. His friends thought he refused to name his tailor because he hoped the fellow wouldn't be overrun with traffic. He couldn't tell them his clothes were all secondhand, bought from a discrete shop near the waterfront and tailored by a seamstress who had worked for his mother. The new pair of boots on his feet were the first to truly fit him in years.

"I am not impoverished," he told her. "But neither am I so plump in the pocket that I can afford to lavish money on this estate. Besides, I was born and raised in London. That is my home."

She met his gaze. "People change their homes, when they find something better."

"Then why have you and your father never left?" he challenged, leaning closer. "Why stay here?"

She smiled. "Because it seems you and I disagree

on the term 'better,' sir. I cannot see any place as better than Blackcliff."

"Truly?" He regarded her, mystified. "Have you no ambitions for a better position for your father? Perhaps your own family one day?"

Her gaze skittered away from his to where her fingers toyed with the end of Dolly's leash. "I thought I might find that here."

He could think of no man he'd met who'd be worthy of her. Frustration pushed his tongue. "And are there so many Allbridges in the churchyard?"

She glanced up at him, tears beading her cinnamon-colored lashes. "Just one."

For a moment, guilt kept back anything he might have said, and he could only look into her dark eyes as a tear slid down her cheek. He reached out and stroked it away, and her eyes widened. There was nothing for it. He gathered her against him, holding her gently, meaning only to comfort her. Yet the pounding of his heart told him it at least thought otherwise.

So did Dolly, it seemed, for she lumbered to her feet, a growl reverberating out of her throat. He felt it through his boots. He released Gwen immediately.

She obviously knew her dog better, for she was staring toward the open door of the withdrawing room, and so was the mastiff.

"Someone's out there," Gwen whispered.

Chapter Thirteen

Gwen saw nothing moving outside the door, yet she was certain Dolly knew otherwise. Trevor must have thought so, too, for he reached for his cane and swung himself to his feet.

"Stay here," he hissed to Gwen.

She refused. Blackcliff was her home; no one threatened it. She bent and removed the leash from Dolly's collar.

"Go," she said, standing and pointing to the door.

Dolly went, paws pounding over the floor, bark rattling the sconces on the wall. Trevor and Gwen hurried after, Trevor leaning on his cane.

Dolly bound down the corridor, each leap carrying her yards. Rearing up on her back paws, she braced her front paws on the door to the servants' stair. Her demanding barks boomed against the paneling. Gwen rushed up to her and slipped the leash back onto her collar, even as Mrs. Bentley came puffing from the other end of the house.

"What's happened?" the housekeeper cried as Gwen ordered Dolly down off the door.

"Dolly's cornered someone," Trevor replied, and Gwen could hear the excitement in his voice. It seemed he loved the chase as much as Dolly did. He reached for the door and threw it open. Gwen tensed.

But inside, on the landing, the shepherd statue sat serenely.

Gooseflesh pricked her arms, and Mrs. Bentley sucked in a breath. Trevor loped past the statue for the outside door.

"Unlatched," he reported. He opened it and gazed out along the graveled path leading to the outbuilding that held the laundry, then glanced back at his housekeeper. "Has anyone worked in the laundry recently?"

"Not since Thursday, Sir Trevor," she said, eyes too wide for Gwen's comfort.

"Then it seems our mysterious visitor has been here." He shut the door and locked it, then turned to the statue. "Mrs. Bentley, forgive me for asking, but could you carry that statue back to the withdrawing room? I want a better look at it."

The housekeeper swallowed but nodded.

Their progress down the corridor was much slower than their journey up. Mrs. Bentley was lugging the statue and holding it so far away from her generous chest that Gwen thought she'd surely over-balance.

But Gwen had her hands full with Dolly. The mastiff kept glancing back the way they had come and whining, and Gwen gripped the leash tightly lest the dog decide to bolt for the stairs again. Sir Trevor moved slowest of all, leaning heavily on his borrowed cane. Gwen could only hope he had done himself no permanent injury.

He sank onto the chair as soon as they reached it and swung his feet up onto the embroidered foot-stool he had been using. He could not quite hide his grimace.

"If you'd put the statue on the table here, Mrs. Bentley," he said.

Gwen ordered Dolly to stay, then helped the housekeeper place the statue beside Trevor. Mrs. Bentley scurried back as if she couldn't wait to get away from it, but Trevor narrowed his eyes as if taking in even the grain of the fine white marble.

"What's so special about this that our visitor continues to return to it?" he mused aloud. His gaze jumped to meet Gwen's. "Cord said it was from France. Do you know anything else about it?"

Gwen shrugged. "Not really. And I don't remember it moving about before you arrived, despite what Mr. Cord said. It's been part of the house as long as I can remember. See? The base is built from the same wood as all the paneling."

He nodded.

"It's very like the statue of the Lord in St. Martin's," Mrs. Bentley put in, stepping a little closer to the table as if linking the statue to godly things eased her concerns. "That came from some foreign place."

"Italy, I think," Gwen agreed. "Though I imagine the colonel might have been able to purchase it in France, as Mr. Cord said."

"So a costly piece," Trevor said, one finger rubbing his square chin. "Yet our villain never steals it. He merely moves it about."

"Perhaps he means to steal it but keeps getting interrupted," Gwen offered. She bent to pat Dolly's head, and the mastiff's tail thumped once against the ruby carpet.

"Nothing stood between him and freedom this time," Trevor pointed out. "He could easily have carried it out the door with him."

"Oh, not so, sir," Mrs. Bentley protested, hands fluttering before her white apron. "I wouldn't want to run carrying that thing!"

Trevor nodded. "So we are looking for a small man or a woman."

Despite herself, Gwen bristled. "This is ridiculous! No man or woman in the village would steal from Blackcliff Hall!"

"Then you think they move the statue for some other purpose?" he asked with a frown.

In truth, she wasn't sure what to think. The statue

couldn't move on its own, but she could find no reason for anyone to move it.

"It's a puzzle to be sure," Mrs. Bentley said with a sigh.

Trevor raised his head as if she'd said something insightful. "Mrs. Bentley, send Dorie out to Rob and have him carry this up to my bedchamber. Leave it beside the bed. I'll study it more later."

Her round face puckered. "Are you certain, sir? I wouldn't want to sleep in the same room with it."

Trevor reached out to touch her plump hand. "It's only a piece of stone, Mrs. Bentley. It can't hurt us."

With a last doubtful look at the little shepherd, the housekeeper bobbed a curtsy and left.

Gwen knew she should leave. She had no reason to stay. The interviews were over, and Dolly had done her job. She'd be wanted at home to cook her father dinner before he started his rounds. She patted her thigh, and Dolly climbed obligingly to her feet.

"One moment, Gwen," Trevor said, leaning on his cane as if he meant to rise.

"Please don't get up," she said. "You shouldn't have been dashing about to begin with."

He eyed her a moment, then a smile teased his lips. "Doctor's orders, eh?"

She smiled back. "If you like. I'll ask Mrs. Bentley for some more cold compresses before I go."

"And perhaps you could answer me a question, as well."

"Certainly."

He studied her, for all the world as if she were that statue beside him. "Just how badly," he said, "do you wish me to stay?"

Gwen blinked. A dozen answers sprang to mind, all of them unsuitable for a young lady to say to a gentleman. "I've told you how important Blackcliff is to the village, sir."

"Indeed. The last lifeblood it seems. You've gone to great lengths to prove to me how well I'll like it here. Are you setting me a mystery to sweeten the pie?"

A mystery? She'd been right—some part of him relished this challenge with the statue. "I have no part in this, Trevor. Or do you think I'm the one moving the statue?"

"The idea had crossed my mind."

For some reason, the accusation hurt. "Do you truly think me so devious?"

"Not devious," he replied. "But determined."

Was that any better, in his mind? *Lord, give me the words to explain.*

"May I remind you," she said, "that I was here when Dolly heard the noise?"

"Which you could have arranged beforehand. She's well trained—perhaps she even barks on cue."

"Oh, certainly," Gwen said, temper rising. "And the cue would have been me falling into the arms of a handsome gentleman. That's about the only thing I did before she barked."

Was that a blush rising on his cheeks? She'd thought for one moment, when he'd pulled her close, that he had meant to kiss her. Had she been right? But if he had feelings for her, why not stay? He did not seem the type to dally with a woman.

"But you admit you'd do anything to make me stay," he said.

"I admit I wanted you to stay," Gwen replied, "but this presumptuous attitude is not endearing you to me, sir." She gathered the leash close, fully intending to march out the door while she had a shred of dignity left to her.

As if he saw her intentions, he swung himself to his feet and blocked her way. "And you knew nothing about me before I arrived?"

Gwen put her hands on her hips. "What has that to do with anything?"

"Answer the question, please."

Oh, but he could be maddening! "We knew nothing about you, not even your name! And I don't see how that signifies. I had nothing to do with that statue moving, today or in the past. And I am quite put out that you would think otherwise." She angled her nose in the air and tried to avoid his gaze.

He was quiet a moment, then he sighed. "Forgive me, Gwen. I should know there's no guile in you. You have been nothing but kindness itself to me since the day I arrived."

Well, that was better. Gwen lowered her nose and

cast him a glance. He certainly looked contrite with his head hanging. "I have done my best," she said.

"I know." He glanced up at her with an admiring smile. "And your best, my dear, is considerably more than most."

Charm curled around him, as welcoming as the aroma of fresh-baked bread. "You can stop the praises now. You are forgiven."

"And gracious, as well." He took her hand and bowed over it. His touch sent a tremor through her, and she pulled away to rub at her tingling fingers.

"Besides, it seems you had no way of knowing my predilection for solving puzzles."

But she should have guessed. "That's how you won your patent, wasn't it? You solved a puzzle for someone important." She sank back onto the chair, allowing him to do the same. Dolly sat on her haunches beside her.

"Who was it?" Gwen asked. "A member of Parliament? The Prime Minister?"

His mouth quirked in one corner. "Better. A royal duke."

"Oh!" Gwen grinned at him. "No wonder he spoke to the Prince Regent on your behalf."

His smile fled, and the light died in his eyes, leaving them flat. "Guilt will do odd things to a man, even a royal duke. Forgive me for detaining you, Gwen. You were right—all this dashing about has tired me. I think I'll use this excellent cane and toddle on upstairs to my room. Would you ask Mrs. Bentley to bring my supper to me there?"

Gwen nodded and rose once more, but she wasn't fooled. Sir Trevor Fitzwilliam wasn't tired. He wanted to study that statue, to find the person who was moving it. She could only hope that he truly had decided she was innocent.

And that maybe, maybe, this puzzle would give him a reason to stay for a while longer.

Someone was prowling the corridors of Blackcliff unbidden. Trevor couldn't help the current of anticipation that flowed through him like a spring rain. However much he had tried to pretend he was a gentleman and above such things, he still thrilled to every puzzle set before him. He liked matching wits with the enemy and coming out the winner. Even when the enemy was a woman.

He couldn't suspect Gwen for long, worst luck. She would have been a worthy opponent with her boundless energy and endless plans. He'd have truly enjoyed trying to solve any puzzle she set before him.

He'd have liked as much to have her at his side, working with him to figure out who was plaguing Blackcliff. She loved this house, this village, with a passion he could only envy. But he very much feared that danger stalked the footsteps of the little shepherd, so this puzzle was one he intended to solve alone.

The key was the statue. He stared at it, alone in his bedchamber with dinner over and Mrs. Bentley off to bed. Rob had carried the shepherd upstairs and left it on the side table next to Trevor's bed.

The white marble stood out against the crimson bed hangings and the dusky paneling. The nose was chipped where Trevor had collided with the statue on the stairs. The base had been scuffed, but that could easily have been from the times it had been moved about. He still could see no signs of hidden compartments or secret lettering. But he thought he knew a way to get the statue to tell him the truth. Trevor would make their prowler come to him.

He lay the statue on the bed beside him and settled himself to rest.

The fire died in the grate, the red slowly darkening until the glow reminded him of Gwen's hair. She had no idea how lovely she was, how creamy her skin, how deep her eyes. She never hid behind words or teased with her beauty as some of the ladies of London were known to do.

A shame she was so tethered to the village. He could see her at a ball in town, hair dressed, gowned in finest silk. How they would stare when she walked in on his arm.

His arm? He reined in his thoughts. Gwen Allbridge wasn't the woman for him. Much as he admired her looks, much as her character warmed him, his plans called for another type of woman entirely.

He had never been truly accepted in Society. Oh, his father's influence and funding had paid for his education alongside the sons of gentlemen, but there had never been any question about what he was. The stares, the jeers, had cut like chisels, sculpting him into the man he was today. For his children to be spared the humiliation, for his peers to finally see him as one of them, he needed a wealthy wife of impeccable breeding.

His good friend Chase Dearborn, Earl of Allyndale, had offered his sister just this summer. Phoebe Dearborn certainly fit the bill—she was a beauty from a highly respectable family and an heiress in her own right. She was also spoiled and headstrong, and she thought of him as a brother. The announcement of her formal engagement to Algernon Whitaker had only made Trevor breathe a sigh of relief. And no other woman had made him feel the way Gwen did—strong, intelligent, honorable.

His room descended into darkness. Blackcliff Hall settled itself around him. Rain pattered against his window. The sounds, he had to admit, were soothing, homey. A shame Blackcliff didn't come with its own income. He could almost see himself living here.

I go to prepare a place for you. How odd that this verse came to mind. He must be more tired than he thought. No one had ever prepared a place for him. What he had, he owed to his father's guilt and his own determination. Now he just had to see what he could make of them.

The footfall was so muffled by the carpet he barely heard it, yet it set his muscles to tensing. A shadow crept closer to the bed. Trevor adjusted his breathing—in, out, slow and steady, like a man blissfully unaware of the danger looming beside him. A hand reached out for the statue.

Trevor wrapped his fingers around the wrist and yanked. Using the momentum, he rolled himself off the bed and onto his feet, dragging his opponent up onto the bed flat. His sore ankle protested, but he hung on and raised his free hand in a fist. "Who are you? What do you want?"

"Stand down, for God's sake!" Horace Allbridge cried in his rough voice. "I mean no harm!"

Chapter Fourteen

Trevor released his steward and bent to light the brass lamp on the table beside the bed. Allbridge struggled to his feet and stood panting, one gnarled finger tugging at the collar of his worn brown coat, cravat streaming down his chest.

"Explain yourself," Trevor ordered as he straightened.

He nodded shakily. "Just wanted a proper look at the thing. Gwen told me about what happened earlier."

"And you couldn't have waited until tomorrow?" Trevor challenged.

He hung his graying head. "Tomorrow you'd be well enough to ride off, seeing as you're set to leave. Couldn't stand by and watch my girl's heart break."

Gwen, heartbroken? For Blackcliff or Trevor's leaving? And why did the thought that Gwen Allbridge might have feelings for him set him to grinning like a fool? He didn't want to raise her expectations. He wasn't a rake to seduce and abandon a woman.

He forced his face into a scowl. "I fail to see how my leaving should rush your hand. If you meant to steal the thing, you'd have a clearer chance with me gone."

"Ah, but if I'm right, you've no need to go." He raised his head, and, even in the dim light, Trevor could see the eagerness in his pale blue gaze. "I am convinced now that there's money to be had in Blackcliff, Sir Trevor. I'd stake my life on it."

"Money?" Trevor hated the excitement in his voice, even though he knew its cause. "How?"

Allbridge glanced over his shoulder at the statue, lying crooked on the covers. "Reckon that fellow knows the truth of it. That's why someone's out to steal him."

"The statue?" Trevor reached out and dragged it upright. "I've already examined it twice. Is it older than it looks? Was it created by a master?"

Allbridge wrinkled his nose, reminding Trevor of Gwen. "No, worse luck. Brought it with him, Colonel Umbrey did, and never would he be parted from it." He reached for the statue, brows up as if asking permission to touch it.

The story was much like the valet's, but Trevor hesitated a moment before stepping aside and letting his steward lift the shepherd. Allbridge jiggled it up and down, head cocked as if listening.

"He won't give up his secrets so easily," Trevor warned. "I tried."

Allbridge puffed out a sigh as he lowered the statue to the bed. "Perhaps it's not in the statue, then. But there's no mistaking the colonel's legacy."

He glanced toward the door he had left ajar, then lowered his voice. "Brought back all manner of curiosities from his time in India and the Ottoman Empire, the colonel did. This statue, that gold elephant chap in the library, the carved boxes in the dining room." He took a step closer and met Trevor's gaze. "And a fortune in jewels."

"Jewels?" Trevor squelched the hope that sprang up. "There was nothing in the estate records about jewels."

His steward nodded, almost feverishly. "There wouldn't be, now, would there? Old Cornwallis, the Governor-General, he forbid them looting the conquered lands. The colonel must have smuggled them home, a raja's ransom."

The tale still had too many holes for Trevor's liking. "And the solicitor knew nothing?"

Allbridge shook his head. "I feared he did, mind you. Went over the house for days, one room at a time and kept me out of it. I was sure he'd found them and carried them off himself. The fellow certainly put the place up for sale quick enough, and at half its value, I'd say."

Then that's how his father had bought it. A distant estate, cheaply priced—what better way to dispose of an unwanted relative?

"So what makes you think otherwise now?" Trevor asked.

Allbridge pointed to the statue again. "Someone else has been searching the house, using him to hide the fact, most like."

Could it be true? Did this house truly hold the fortune he needed? He couldn't help clutching at the story like a drowning man reached for a dangling rope. "Why didn't you explain all this when you made your initial report?"

"I told you— I thought the jewels were gone. And I never knew where they were kept. Never even knew they existed until the mine was shut down. The colonel had enough money before then that he didn't need to use them."

"Then how do you know he used them later?"

"Because he gave me one to sell in Carlisle." He held up his fist. "Ruby it was, nearly this big. Caused quite a stir when I took it in, but it was enough to keep Blackcliff running for a full year. And there were more, he hinted as much."

Trevor glanced around the room. Somewhere—in a wall? Behind a painting? In a false drawer at the bottom of a wardrobe? In this very room might lie a fortune in jewels, perhaps enough to allow him to achieve his dreams at last. It might be a fool's quest, but how could he walk away without trying?

He grinned at his steward. "Mr. Allbridge, you've

just given me an excellent reason to tarry in Blackcliff."

Allbridge matched his grin. "We can start looking in the morning."

"Why wait?" Trevor countered, heading for the wardrobe. "If there's a fortune in Blackcliff, I mean to find it." He glanced over his shoulder at his steward. "But let's keep this between the two of us. The last thing we need is another fortune hunter."

Gwen hurried up the drive for Blackcliff Hall the next morning, her brown coat heavy about her legs. She'd spent much of the night tossing and turning, worrying about what might be and finding no answers on how she could prevent it. She'd prayed for guidance, for deliverance, for help, but the Lord seemed strangely quiet, and she could not find His peace. She had risen hopeful she might have better luck at services this morning.

But something was up. Her father had come in too late last night and left again early this morning, and with the flimsiest of excuses.

"Estate business," she muttered to Dolly. The mastiff trotted along beside her, head lowered, tail swinging against Gwen's coat. "With Trevor leaving, what business could he have, and on a Sunday morning?"

Dolly woofed as if in agreement. More likely it was the moist scent of the decaying leaves along the drive. It had rained last night, turning the gravel to black and stripping more leaves from the trees to litter the ground with color. Winter was coming. It would be a poor Christmas this year with Blackcliff Hall closed.

She climbed the stairs to the front door and reached for the handle. She should probably go around and come in through the butler's pantry like a proper member of the staff, but she'd never felt like a member of the staff. The colonel had told her not to stand on ceremony, and she didn't see the need to change that now.

Yet the door refused to budge. Locked? Had Trevor left already?

Panic coursed through her, and she pounded on the door. The hard wood stung her hand even through her gloves, and her breath caught in her throat. Dolly began howling at Gwen's agitation. But Gwen couldn't stop. He couldn't leave! He wouldn't abandon her! She needed to say goodbye!

Mrs. Bentley opened the door and gasped as Gwen pushed past her, Dolly at her heels. "Where's Sir Trevor?"

Dolly was already tracking about the floor, nose sniffing against the thick carpet. She set off down the corridor even as Mrs. Bentley said, "In the library with your father, Miss Allbridge."

Gwen nodded her thanks and followed her dog.

Dolly was waiting on her haunches at the library door, tail sweeping across the stone floor. Gwen took a deep breath. She could hear the murmur of voices inside, short and swift. He was here. He hadn't left her. She felt as if she could breathe again. Yet what were they doing? She pushed on the door, but it too was locked.

"Sir Trevor?" she called through the panel. "Father? Is everything all right?"

For a moment, she heard nothing, as if all movement, all speech had frozen. Then came a flurry of sound—thumps, rustlings, scrapes and grunts. "Sir Trevor?" she called again.

The door snicked open, and her father looked out, face red and perspiration beading along his receding hairline.

"All fine here, my girl. Did you have need of me?"

Gwen tried to look beyond him, but he was positioned so that she could see only a thin slice of the library: a corner of the hearth and part of the mantel above it. The painting had been removed; she could spy the empty satin cord dangling from the picture rail above. Why would Trevor redecorate now?

"Are you attending services this morning?" she asked her father. "Or is Sir Trevor planning to travel on the Sabbath?"

"Oh, no need for that," her father said cheerfully. "He's decided to stay a bit longer."

Gwen stared at him, joy rising up until she thought she might lift straight off the stone floor. *Thank You, Lord!* "Oh, Father, truly?"

He winked at her, happier than she'd seen him in

months. "Didn't think your old father had it in him, did you? We'll be out shortly. I'd forgotten about it being Sunday, but we should go to church. We'll soon have cause to be thankful."

"I'll take Dolly back to the gatehouse and wait for you there," Gwen said. But as far as she was concerned, she had cause to be thankful right now.

Trevor found it hard to sit in services that day. For one thing, he itched to keep searching for the jewels. For another, he had decided that he had to say something to the villagers about the Blackcliff Mine. If he found the jewels, he could afford to keep the house open, perhaps even invest in improving the mine so that it would produce a profit again. If he didn't find the jewels, the villagers needed to know that they must look elsewhere for work.

A word in David Newton's ear was enough to earn Trevor a few moments before the congregation was dismissed.

"I want to thank you all for your warm welcome," he started, standing at the front of St. Martin's with the pale stone arches rising on either side of him. Faces gazed back at him, and he recognized many of them: the powerfully built Mr. Casperson, who he'd confirmed as constable; Mr. Agnew the wheelwright, who had perked up the moment Trevor had stepped forward; Squire Lockhart, who looked at Trevor with something approaching respect; Ruth

Newton; and Gwen and her father. Gwen's look of approval buoyed him, and he pushed ahead.

"I know how important the Blackcliff Mine is to this village," he told them all. "I made you a promise when I first arrived about reopening it. Since then, I've had a chance to learn more about the mine. The timbers are in worse shape than I realized. We will need a considerable amount of funds to make the mine safe for you to work in it again. I do not have access to those funds at the present, but I'm working to rectify that matter."

Disappointment flittered across a few faces, but for the most part they nodded as if appreciating his predicament. Trevor took a deep breath.

"If I fail to find those funds, the mine will not reopen. I will let you all know as soon as I know more. Thank you for your time."

He waited for a moment, expecting complaints, shouts of frustration and blame. Instead, the good people of Blackcliff looked at each other, then turned their faces to the cross. As Trevor returned to his seat, David Newton led them in a final prayer. Their voices rose in thanks and praise, and everyone filed out in good humor. Trevor had never seen anything like it.

"Well done, lad," the squire said, passing him outside the church. "Your father would be proud."

For some reason, the reminder of his father did not sting as much as it had in the past.

The next few days flew by. Trevor and Horace

Allbridge took one room at a time. They rapped every wall, checked behind all paintings, moved furniture and rugs, opened each decorative box and peered into individual silver and porcelain vases. They found any number of interesting things, from a gold button with a paste diamond in the center to an odd-shaped hook Allbridge claimed women used to crochet doilies. Unfortunately, they failed to locate any cache of jewels on the main floor.

More tricky, however, was hiding their work. Mrs. Bentley was concerned they weren't eating enough, so she could appear at any time with a tray of biscuits and tea or some sliced cheese. Trevor was getting quite adept at turning her away. His steward suggested searching at night, but Trevor wanted more light to make sure they overlooked nothing. So, Allbridge let it be known they were inventorying the Hall, which gave them every reason to closet themselves away during the day.

However, it also gave Gwen reason to offer her help, and she wasn't easy to dissuade. At first Trevor sent her on this errand and that—for parchment from the village to make lists, for more ointment for his ankle. But she was far too efficient and always returned, successful, in far too short a time to do him any good.

It would have been easier if Trevor could have confided in her. The urge to do so was strong. He could imagine the glow in her dark eyes, her pretty mouth pursed in an O of appreciation when she learned the house might hold a fortune in jewels. But he could also imagine the light fading, her face puckering, if her father's tale proved false. She put such faith in Blackcliff; he could not see her disappointed again. No, until he knew he had the jewels, he had to keep Gwen in the dark.

By the third day, all his gambits seemed too feeble, and he knew the best way to keep Gwen from learning the truth was to distract her himself. When she arrived with her father, he immediately drew her aside.

"I wonder if you might assist me this morning, Miss Allbridge."

She dimpled up at him, and he hated that he'd given her no true cause. "Certainly, sir."

He tapped the cane against the side of his boot. He didn't need the crutch anymore; his ankle rarely pained him. But there was something distinguished about swinging that ebony stick.

"I find myself tired of these walls. Would you be available this morning for a tour of the village? I don't believe we saw all its glories the day we confirmed everyone."

She agreed readily, and a short time later, they were strolling down the lane to the village.

He hadn't really looked at the place any of the times he'd journeyed through it, but he wasn't surprised to find it consisted of several rough stone buildings clustered along a main street and snug two-story houses behind and at either end. Some of the buildings had been whitewashed, but most still bore the mottled look of the gray-and-black stones from the fell.

Yet Gwen's attitude must have rubbed off on him, for everywhere he looked he saw signs of care and beauty: flower boxes under the windows overflowed with the last dusky buds of autumn, the air was scented with roasting meat. Tall Mr. Williamson tipped his hat in respect, wooden box tucked under the arm of his tweed coat, as he hurried toward the church.

On the corner of the lane, Ruth Newton was crouched beside a group of rapt children, with no care for the dirt brushing her fine skirts. Their high voices rose in a song that brought a smile to her face, making her appear younger, prettier. She still blushed when she caught Trevor's gaze on her.

Gwen took it all in stride, smiling at this person, waving to another. This was her place, her people, and Trevor could only envy her that. He felt as if the village, the church, even the mountain were calling to him. A shame he could not be sure of his answer.

Chapter Fifteen

Trevor had to admit that the village was more interesting than he'd suspected. Perhaps it was because he had such a charming guide.

"There's the market," Gwen explained, pointing to a long, low building near the church. "People from all around bring goods and food in on Tuesdays during the summer months."

"And the other months of the year?" Trevor teased.

She elbowed him good-naturedly. "Who needs to eat the other months, Sir Glutton?"

He laughed as she steered him to a little shop next door to the George. The multipaned windows were crowded with everything from a high-crowned beaver hat to a bushel of rosy apples. Inside, the store was narrow and deep, but a wooden chandelier overhead shed warm light on wares that were just as eclectic. One wall was obscured by bolts of bright muslin and warm wool, and the other was filled with produce and tools of various kinds. The oily scent of beeswax mixed with the dry scent of tea. Trevor recognized the burly fellow behind the high counter at the back as the village constable.

"Mr. Casperson," Gwen greeted him. "I was just showing Sir Trevor where to buy whatever his heart desires."

Casperson rocked from his heels to the balls of his feet and back again. "My pleasure to serve, sir, though in all fairness I must say that Mrs. Delaney has a fine shop just around the corner for papers and ink and books and such. Imports them all the way from London."

"Such a distance," Trevor marveled with a conspiratorial wink to Gwen.

"Oh, we spare no expense, sir," the shopkeeper said, bulbous nose high with his own regard. "We are the purveyors of culture here in Blackcliff."

"Mr. Casperson also arranges the assemblies in the market hall," Gwen explained.

"Indeed, indeed," he boomed. He made a great show of rearranging the tea canisters on his pocked wooden counter. "And speaking of which, Miss Allbridge, I wondered whether you would be gracing us with your presence this Saturday. I for one would appreciate seeing your smiling face across the line in a dance."

The fellow was recommending himself to her. Trevor felt the urge to step between them, assert his place. But that was ridiculous; he had no right to such behavior when it came to Gwen Allbridge.

She scrunched up her nose. "You are too kind, Mr. Casperson, but I'm not sure my father will be up to it."

The words were out before he knew it. "If you feel the need for an escort, Miss Allbridge, I would be happy to oblige."

Casperson ogled him, mouth agape. Gwen looked nearly as surprised. "Why, how kind, Sir Trevor. I'd be honored."

"Good," he said, feeling ridiculously pleased with himself. "It's settled, then. I suppose I'll need to talk to the cobbler about dancing shoes. In the meantime, perhaps you could be so good as to provide us with a few of those apples, Mr. Casperson. I suddenly find myself ravenous."

Sir Trevor Fitzwilliam was escorting her to the assembly! The masters of Blackcliff had rarely condescended in the past, although Squire Lockhart generally came for a short while as a courtesy. The thought of attending on Trevor's arm made Gwen feel like an enchanted princess in the stories her mother had read her as a child, as if she'd woken from a deep sleep to find the world a bright and wonderful place. Everything had to be simply perfect! So, she set about making it so.

She enlisted Ruth Newton's aid in altering a dress for the assembly, buying a length of velvet for an overskirt. She spoke with Mr. Casperson about the arrangements, then set about improving them with his grudging permission.

The quartet he had hired to play was quite fine, but Gwen talked Rob Winslow into building a raised dais for them to play on and then hung bunting about it as well as the whitewashed walls of the market hall. She worked with Mrs. Delaney to polish the floors until she could see her reflection in the old wood. The only difficulty in all her work was that it kept her away from the Hall.

"We'll get along without you," her father assured her when she lamented over dinner one night. "Sir Trevor and I have plenty to keep us busy. You have a higher calling right now."

Gwen felt it, too. Her prayers seemed to be reaching heaven again, for everything went exactly as she hoped.

She wanted this to be the best assembly Blackcliff had ever hosted. She encouraged all the women to bring their best cider, pastries, cheeses and fruits for the refreshment table. She even convinced Mr. Casperson to provide real beeswax candles for the brass chandeliers that lighted the huge hall and David Newton to loan a number of fine chairs from St. Martin's to line the walls.

"I've never seen the place so lovely," Mrs. Delaney marveled the afternoon of the assembly as they finished putting the final touches on the room.

"You are to be congratulated, Miss Allbridge. You've worked hard for this day."

Gwen knew she should be tired, but she felt full of life, full of joy, for the first time in a long time. As she tweaked the last curl into place beside her face that night, she thought she might glow just as much as Mr. Casperson's candles. She spun in a circle, watching her gown twirling about her ankles.

"A picture you look," her father said from the doorway.

Gwen turned to him and felt her smile evaporating. "Why aren't you dressed? You said you'd come this time."

He waved a hand. "You've no need for me along to enjoy yourself."

"That is not the point, and you know it." She advanced on him. "You're Blackcliff's steward again. That changes everything."

"Doesn't change how I feel," he protested stubbornly. "A dance is no place for me without your mother."

Gwen put out a hand and touched his tense arm. "She would have wanted you to go on living, Father."

"And you, as well. Yet you won't even make her syrup."

Gwen pulled back. "That's not the same thing at all. I simply don't want to get it wrong."

He snorted. "You've never gotten a recipe wrong in your life. Admit it—you miss her, too."

"Of course I miss her! The house seems too large, my contribution too small. But we cannot continue on like this, Father!"

He patted her shoulder. "Now, then, don't upset yourself. Go and have a grand time with Sir Trevor."

In the end, that was all she could do.

She had her dancing shoes in a cloth bag and her walking shoes on under her cloak when there was a rap at the door. She threw it open with a ready smile, only to find a stranger on her doorstep. He was tall, with a long nose, powdered wig and gilt buttons on his royal blue coat.

"Squire Lockhart and Sir Trevor Fitzwilliam of Blackcliff request the presence of Miss Gwendolyn Allbridge," he intoned to the air above her head.

Gwen peered around him to find Trevor grinning at her from the window of a fine carriage. Four horses, white as snow, waited regally for her in front of the hunter-green coach. The footman went ahead of her and threw open the door, but it was Sir Trevor who reached for her hand and helped her into the gracious interior.

"Welcome, Miss Allbridge," the squire said from beside Sir Trevor. They had both seated themselves in the rear-facing bench so that she might have the place of honor facing forward. The squire's sturdy frame was covered in black, from his flowing cape to his breeches and patent shoes. His cravat and stockings were as white as his horses.

"How kind of you to take me up," Gwen said to him.

"Couldn't refuse Sir Trevor's request," the squire said with a look of amusement to Trevor. "He seemed to think you deserved a coach and outriders, at the very least. This was the best I could do."

Gwen thanked him again, then turned her smile on Trevor. His multicaped greatcoat hid all but his stockings and the black shoes he'd ordered from the cobbler for the occasion, yet, to her mind, his ready smile made him all the more presentable as the coach set off for the village.

Theirs was one of the only carriages discharging before the door of the market hall. Wagons and carts crowded the lane, and Mr. Billings at the George had opened his stables for the waiting horses. Other people made their way on foot, ladies lifting their hems and gentlemen stepping around puddles. Lanterns blazed on either side of the wide door, and light and noise streamed out each time it opened to admit another group.

Inside, Gwen and Trevor pulled off their outer garments and hung them from pegs with the others. Turning, she found Sir Trevor staring at her.

She plucked at the green-velvet overskirt, lifting it off the pale white muslin of the gown. She'd thought she looked rather well in the short, puffed sleeves and lace-edged square neck. "It was my mother's. Ruth altered it for me."

"My esteem for Miss Newton's talents continues

to increase," he said. "But then, the gown is only as lovely as the woman wearing it."

Gwen beamed. "Many more of these compliments, sir, and you will quite turn my head."

"Then I shall count my work as finished, my dear."

Gwen excused herself a moment and went to the ladies' retiring room to change into her dance slippers. When she returned to Trevor's side, she found the market hall was already crowded. So many people thronged the cavernous space that she could barely make out the decorations.

Gwen adored their quarterly assemblies. Everyone fifteen years or older in the parish was welcome to attend, and families from as far away as the lower part of the valley had been known to join in. Along the far wall, Mrs. Delaney was making use of the chairs from St. Martin's to talk with Rob Winslow's father, the blacksmith. Ruth Newton—in a dashing muslin gown with a modest neck edged in lace and the hem trimmed in pale pink ribbon—was serving cider to one of the squire's tenants at the refreshment table along the back.

Gwen knew everyone by name, had grown up among them, had dosed many of them since her mother's passing. As Sir Trevor led her around the room, her neighbors paused in their conversations to nod, dip curtsies, or bow in respect.

She knew it wasn't her that they acknowledged with such deference. It was the man beside her.

She'd thought Trevor Fitzwilliam magnificent the day he had arrived. Tonight, in his black-velvet coat and dove-gray breeches, he was beyond magnificent. He stood taller than any other man in the room. His green eyes were bright with wit and merriment; his dark hair gleamed in the candlelight. The ladies whispered behind their fans as he passed, and their gazes followed him around the room.

Oh, how she'd have liked to keep him to herself all night, but that would hardly be proper. Besides, she knew having the master of Blackcliff here meant a great deal to everyone. She dared not monopolize his time, but at least she could offer him her first dance.

She loved dancing, too: the spritely rhythm of the music from the quartet, the twirl and march of the steps, the thrill of catching a look from her partner as they passed in the center of the figure. She clapped and promenaded and stepped back and forth and to and fro, her skirts swishing about her.

"You are in fine looks tonight, if I may say so, Miss Allbridge," Mr. Casperson said when she and Sir Trevor progressed past him in the dance.

"Thank Ruth Newton and your fine establishment," Gwen replied with a grin. "She did the work and you supplied the material."

She took Sir Trevor's hands and danced with him back up the line. His smile was all for her, and suddenly it seemed the music faded, the calling voices stilled, until he was her entire world.

When had that happened?

Gwen stumbled, and he caught her up and turned her back into her place at the top of the line.

"All right, my dear?" he asked with a smile.

Gwen could only nod. She was in love with Trevor. And why not? He challenged her, made her think about her actions. Until he'd come into her life, she hadn't realized how many of the gentlemen in Blackcliff merely bowed to her wishes, regardless of whether her actions were the best for all concerned. Trevor was made of stronger stuff.

Could he love her in return? She'd wanted him to love Blackcliff for the villagers' sake, for her father's sake. What if he loved it for her sake?

What if he loved her?

Her face was blazing, and she knew it wasn't from her exertions. As soon as the set ended, she hurried for a chair.

"Are you all right?" he asked again, following her, dark brows knit in concern.

Gwen waved a hand. "Fine. Just a bit winded."

He shook his head. "You are the most energetic woman I have ever met. I cannot believe a set of dances affected you."

She could not tell him the truth, that it was his presence that was affecting her. "Even *I* get winded, sir. But you needn't sit out with me if you'd prefer to dance. I'm sure any number of ladies would be delighted to accompany you."

His frown deepened. "How could I enjoy myself

knowing you were unwell? Let me bring you something to drink." He strode off before she could disagree.

Gwen put a shaky hand to her head. She had to get ahold of herself. Trevor deserved to enjoy the evening, and her thoughts, swirling faster than her skirts, were not going to spoil everyone's hard work. By the time he returned, she was smiling pleasantly and could accept the cider he offered with a polite word of thanks.

"Go on," she urged when he looked as if he would hover. "I'll be fine, I promise."

He glanced around the room, which had only grown more crowded. So many couples had stood up to dance that four lines had been formed. "I'll never find you again in all this."

"Nonsense," Gwen said with a grin. "I'm the only redhead in Blackcliff, and you are the tallest man here. We couldn't possibly miss each other."

He smiled at that, and her heart leaped inside her. "If you're certain."

"I'm certain. I would not want it said I kept you all to myself."

He took her free hand and bowed over it. "Only know that you keep my heart." He straightened and strolled off.

Oh, but she must be blushing again. She felt warm all over. How did Ruth bear it as oft as her face flushed? And how could Gwen bear it if Trevor left? He would be taking her heart with him.

Chapter Sixteen

Trevor was hard-pressed to remember such a fine evening. Oh, he'd visited assembly rooms before. The cotton bunting and old wood floor were no match for the classical elegance of Almack's in London. The food on the other hand, was far superior, and he thought he'd surely eaten his weight in pastries that night alone.

Certainly he'd been to balls before, some of which held far more people with enough flashes of silk and jewels to blind him. Conversations, however, were shallow, wit piled on wit with little substance to sustain it. The Blackcliff assembly had wit aplenty, but conversation inevitably wound around to who was missing from the previous quarter, how to help and what must be done to bring everyone safely through to the next assembly. The dance, it seemed, was one of the few places where the leaders of the valley gathered, and far more than dancing went on.

Certainly he'd met his share of notables: princes, royal dukes, the titled and the wealthy. For all but a few, he'd been the oddity, someone to puzzle over at best and dismiss with scorn at worst. But in Blackcliff, he was the royalty, his opinion sought and heeded, his character praised.

Certainly he'd danced with beautiful women before, their husky laughter and sweet perfume teasing him. None of them made him feel the way Gwen Allbridge did—alive, awakened, appreciated. She truly had captured his heart.

He simply didn't know what to do about it.

She was quiet as they drove home, the light from the lanterns outside making streaks of fire in her hair. He wanted to reach out, to stroke his hands down the satiny strands to see if they felt as warm as they looked. But he feared he'd overstepped his bounds already tonight with his declaration, and the squire was present although nodding off in the corner.

Still, it was all he could do not to gather her in his arms when he helped her down at the gatehouse. He tried to satisfy himself by holding her hand far longer than was necessary. "Thank you, Gwen, for a wonderful evening."

"Thank you," she insisted. "That was the best assembly ever held in Blackcliff!"

"Only because of you," he said. He might not

have had the right to kiss her lips, but he brought her hand up and pressed a kiss against her glove. A noticeable tremor ran up her arm; he felt as if it ran through him, as well.

"Good night, Gwen," he murmured, meeting her sweet gaze.

"Good night, Trevor."

He watched until she was safely inside.

"Bellows to mend, eh, old fellow?" the squire said as Trevor climbed back into the carriage for the ride up the drive.

Trevor sighed. "Miss Allbridge would make a fine wife, but I never intended to make Blackcliff my home."

"Indeed?" Lockhart leaned forward. The light from the coach's lanterns gleamed on his silver hair. "Your father gave me the impression you intended to settle here."

Trevor did not want to feel angry, not tonight. "You speak with my father far more frequently than I do, I'm sure."

The squire nodded. "Less than you think. Not much of a correspondent, your father, but he can make himself known when he wishes."

Bitterness was clawing its way up his throat, and Trevor struggled to contain it. "I wouldn't know about that."

"His actions may seem harsh," the squire said. "But you must understand. He was young, scarcely ten and seven when he met your mother. And she was not the first with whom he'd fancied himself in love."

Or the last. London was rife with gossip about his father and the actress with whom he was now living. "He paid for my education," Trevor said, face feeling stiff. "For that I owe him a debt. But I cannot like that he exiled me to Blackcliff."

The squire leaned back against the squabs. "Perhaps you'll change your mind in time. But if you are determined to return to London, you'd do worse than to take Miss Allbridge as your bride. She'd do well in the capital, I think."

He had felt the same, but he knew the impediments. "Only if she'd consent to leave the valley."

"Ah. She is rather devoted to the place, isn't she? But wives follow their husbands. That is the way of the world."

The squire couldn't know that Blackcliff was Gwen's world. Her life, her heart, belonged here. Like an exotic flower, would she bloom anywhere else? Or wither and die?

Lockhart let Trevor off in front of Blackcliff Hall and had his driver wheel the coach and head into the night. Trevor climbed the stairs slowly, still thinking about Gwen. She wasn't indifferent to him; her warm smiles and blushes told him as much. Would she be willing to leave the valley and all she knew behind for him? Was he willing to ask it of her? How could he afford a wife if they never found the jewels?

The moment he opened the door, he knew something was wrong. The carpet in the entryway had been pulled up and tossed aside. Decorative tables in the withdrawing room had been toppled, their contents spilling onto the floor or missing entirely.

"Mrs. Bentley?" Trevor called, moving toward the butler's pantry and the door to the kitchen. "Allbridge?"

Someone groaned.

Trevor tore into the pantry and skidded to a stop. The drawers holding the flatware lay open, the silver littering the floor and the body of a man spread out on the stones. The articles missing from the withdrawing room lay scattered about. Worst of all was the smell, as if someone had opened a gin shop in the room.

Horace Allbridge opened an eye and sighted on Trevor. "Ah, Sir Trevor." His croaky voice was slurred. "Back so soon?"

"Not soon enough, apparently," Trevor said, crouching beside him. "What happened here?"

Allbridge waved a hand. "We've been had, Sir Trevor. Life is nothing but misery. We might as well get used to it." He closed both eyes again and sagged against the cabinets.

"Allbridge!" Trevor put his ear to his steward's chest and was relieved to hear the steady beat of his heart. Rising, he glanced around again. How had Horace Allbridge come to be in the pantry? Had he surprised a thief? Or had he, in a drunken stupor, decided to steal from his master?

He didn't want to think of his steward as a thief. The past few days, they'd become partners of a sort. He'd come to appreciate the man's dry humor, his insights. Trevor wanted to trust him, to believe the best of him, but doubts kept raising their heads, like crows awakening, and Trevor could not shake them.

Allbridge had been missing the night Trevor had arrived. Had he been drunk or hiding evidence of previous thefts? Trevor had never been given an inventory of the house. How could he know what else might have been in Blackcliff before he arrived?

When Allbridge had made his first report, he'd advised Trevor to leave for London. Had he been trying to get Trevor out of the house before Trevor discovered other thefts? As the steward with full access to Blackcliff, Horace Allbridge had many opportunities to move the statue. Could he have been trying to scare Trevor away? And when Trevor had caught him that night in the bedchamber, the man could have made up the story of the jewels to save himself from Trevor's wrath.

Whichever way Trevor looked at it, his steward had a lot of explaining to do. But how was Trevor to explain that to Gwen?

Gwen was having a difficult time heading for bed again. Still gowned in her fine dress, she sat on the little wooden stool in front of the mirror on her dressing table, brush in hand, staring at her reflection but not really seeing it. Her mind kept turning on the events of the evening: how handsome Trevor had looked, how attentive he'd been, how he'd gazed at her when he had brought her home, so tenderly. She'd thought he meant to kiss her at last.

She'd wanted him to kiss her.

Father, what a blessing it would be for Trevor to love me!

Over the years, she'd had any number of suitors, all young men from the valley. Rob Winslow had been hanging after her since they were twelve. At first, she had refused to take them seriously because they seemed like puppies playing in the farmyard, all noise and affection. Once her mother had become ill, Gwen had focused on helping around the house, on trying to cure her, on keeping the disease from spreading.

Then her mother had died, and her father had crawled inside a gin bottle, and she'd turned her attentions to him. And just as he began to improve, Colonel Umbrey had passed on, plunging the village into despair. She couldn't stand by and do nothing. She had to help. But all that helping left little time to fall in love, until now.

Lord, show me what You want me to do. It's so easy to be drawn to Trevor. But is he the one You meant for me?

She had scarcely finished the prayer when someone knocked on the door. Oh, not a sickness, tonight of all nights! Yet how many times had her mother answered that knock, cures in hand, ready to leave hearth and family when needed? Gwen could do no less. She dropped the brush on the table and hurried to answer.

Rob Winslow stood on the step, his face drawn.

Gwen felt as if the breath had stopped in her chest. "Is it Sir Trevor? Did he fall again?"

He shook his head. "It's your father. Sir Trevor found him in the house in a terrible state."

Her stomach roiled. "I'll get Mother's cures."

He grabbed her arm to keep her from moving. "They won't help him now. Sir Trevor's sent me for the constable."

"What?" Gwen shook herself, trying to focus. "Why?"

He dropped his gaze and his hand. "Your father was found in the butler's pantry with the silver in his hands."

No! Her father wouldn't steal. "There must be a reason."

Rob's look was sad, as if he pitied her. "Perhaps, but it doesn't look good. I thought you should know." He took a step back.

"Wait!" Gwen snatched her cloak off the hook by the door. "Give me a few minutes. I'll talk to Sir Trevor."

"I've got to do my duty," Rob protested. "This job is too important to my family. I want to give the master reason to hire me permanently."

"I know." Gwen followed him out the door. "Just slow your steps a little. That's all I ask."

Rob nodded, smile turning up. "I can do that. Watch yourself, now. And I hope you know that if you need anything..."

Gwen squeezed his arm. "I know. Thank you."

She hesitated only long enough to assure herself that her father's lantern wasn't in its usual place by the front door. She hadn't noticed it when she'd returned, either; she'd assumed he and Dolly were out on their rounds about the estate. How had he come to be in the butler's pantry? And where was Dolly?

There was enough moon, riding high among scudding clouds, for her to pick her way up the drive to the front of the Hall. The gravel crunched against her shoes, but the sounds were not as loud as her thoughts. Her father had been acting strangely lately—hiding away in various rooms of the Hall, refusing to go to the assembly tonight when he'd promised her weeks ago he would accompany her. Yet stealing? Never!

Lamps burned on either side of Blackcliff's door as she approached, and light blazed from the withdrawing-room window. Perhaps Trevor had already realized his mistake, and she could take her father home to his bed.

She climbed the stairs and opened the door. "Sir Trevor?" she called as she moved into the entryway.

Somewhere to her right a word was bitten back in frustration. Trevor strode into the entryway from the withdrawing room. He still wore his greatcoat, and his shoulders seemed to fill the doorway. His face was tight, his lips compressed.

"Go home, Gwen," he said, and it was an order.

Gwen's heart sank even as her spine stiffened. "Rob said you had my father."

He puffed out a breath. "Of course Rob told you. You command loyalties, even mine."

He sounded saddened by that fact. "You command loyalties, as well. Everyone welcomed you at the assembly tonight."

"Everyone except your father. It seems he had something else in mind."

His voice was flat, yet the words hit like stones, leaving a dull ache. "My father would never steal from Blackcliff. What happened?"

He eyed her a moment as if choosing his words carefully. "Did you know your father has trouble holding his drink?"

The question caught her off guard. "Not anymore!"

He raised a brow. "Indeed." He turned aside and motioned to the withdrawing room. "Perhaps you would care to explain, then."

Gwen was almost afraid of what she'd find in the room, but she forced herself to cross in front of him and peer inside. Her father sat slumped in one of the leather-bound chairs, eyes closed, clothes rumpled. Once more she felt as if the air had been knocked from her. She rushed to his side and bent over him. The stench of gin singed her nostrils.

Tears burned. "Oh, Father."

His eyes opened, bloodshot and puffy. "Now, now. S'not so bad." His voice was thick. "Only had cup or two to ward off the chill." His eyes fluttered closed again.

"I should never have left him." She wiped damp hair off his moist face with her fingers. "He'd been doing so well. He hasn't had a night like this in weeks."

"You are not his keeper," Trevor said behind her, and she realized his tone had gentled.

"I should have guessed." She turned to look at Trevor. His face was still drawn, haunted. Why did her father's condition hurt him? "He was in despair tonight," she explained. "The dance reminded him of Mother. She loved to dance."

"This isn't just melancholy." He was struggling with something; his mouth opened, closed, then opened again. "Tell me, Gwen. Why did you accompany me to the assembly tonight?"

Gwen frowned. "You ask the oddest questions."

He took a step closer, gaze drilling down into hers as if he needed to see inside her. "I ask questions that need to be answered. Why did you want me at the assembly? Did your father encourage you to go?"

"Certainly. He wanted me to enjoy the evening."

He stiffened as if she'd struck him. What was

wrong with him? Where was the kind, caring man who'd been loath to leave her side all evening? Had she mistaken him even then?

She had done everything to make Trevor the master of Blackcliff. Now it seemed her father was to pay the price for her efforts.

Chapter Seventeen

Trevor's next words only served to confuse Gwen further.

"And what do you know of Colonel Umbrey's jewels?" he asked, watching her.

Had the world turned inside out, and she hadn't noticed? "What jewels?"

He glanced at her father as if he expected corroboration of the story. "A fortune in gemstones the colonel smuggled home from India."

Gwen snorted. "A fine story. But if Colonel Umbrey had had a fortune, why did he sell off the horses and carriage? Why didn't he improve the mine? Why let Mr. Cord go when he'd been the colonel's valet for ages?"

His broad shoulders slumped, as if she'd deprived him of his last hope. Waves of emotions crossed his face—disappointment, disgust, despair. He took a deep breath and turned away as if to keep her from seeing more. "Go home, Gwen. We will discuss what to do about all this in the morning."

Gwen refused to budge. She didn't understand the change in him, and her heart felt slashed and bleeding, but she couldn't leave her father. "But you sent Rob for Mr. Casperson. Surely you wouldn't jail my father for one misstep."

"One misstep?" He turned to meet her gaze once more, face so hard he looked like a different man entirely. "Drunk while on duty, stealing from his master, lying about the contents of the house to avoid being caught. I call that sufficient reason to send for the constable."

"My father would never steal. Nor would he lie."

His bearing was equally stiff. "Gwen, I do not want to talk to you about this. He is your father—of course you must defend him."

"He is your steward. Why aren't *you* defending him?"

A muscle was working in his strong jaw. "It's hard to defend against what I've seen tonight. I found him in the butler's pantry with the silver in his hands. Items from the withdrawing room were scattered about him, as if he'd been carrying them away as well when he fell. He offers no explanation. That's incriminating evidence."

She could see how it might be, for another man. "But you know you can trust him. He's had months to steal from the house, and he never has."

"And I have only your word for that. The solicitor gave the inventory to the man who purchased the estate. My benefactor did not think to provide it to me before I came north. Blackcliff could have been filled with treasures before I arrived."

She drew herself up. "So you don't trust me, either?"

He closed his eyes as if he couldn't bear to look at her. "I want to trust you, Gwen, more than you can know. But you love your father. He's all you have. It's possible you would lie to save him."

She wanted to argue, but she knew he was right. "True."

He opened his eyes as if surprised she'd agree so easily. "There's more. Your father could have put that statue across the stairs so I'd fall. He could have been the person Dolly chased down the corridor."

"Barking all the time?" Gwen challenged.

He shrugged. "Her barks could have been excitement for her master rather than determination to catch a stranger."

He could be right there, as well. Dolly's barks always boomed, but she had not growled in warning except for the moment when she'd first been surprised by the sound in the corridor. It was possible she'd known who was hiding there. Yet Gwen could not believe that person had been her father.

"True," she allowed again, "but why would my father do such a thing? We wanted you here. You know that."

"You wanted me here, Gwen. You thought Blackcliff could help the village. At first, your father advised me to leave. Then, when I started studying the statue's movements, he told me the story about the jewels."

"That's what you've been doing," Gwen realized. "You've been searching each room, trying to find those jewels."

He nodded, a little shamefaced, she thought. "But now it appears there are no jewels, and your father merely used the story to throw me off the scent and keep me busy."

Gwen put her hands on her hips. "Oh, certainly. Thieves love to keep their victims in the house they intend to rob."

"You did attend the assembly with me tonight."

She recoiled. "What? Is that why you asked me that question?"

Oh, he was definitely defensive. "Yes. You must see it is a logical assumption."

"Are you blind?" When he blinked in obvious surprise, Gwen rounded on him. "You are the most handsome man I have ever met, and I have made no secret of the fact that I admire and respect you. Add that to the fact that I want you to think the best of the village. Of course the only reason I'd go to an assembly with you is for larcenous purposes."

"I didn't mean…" he started, but Gwen was not about to stop. She advanced on him, and he retreated until he bumped against the paneled wall.

"You want evidence?" Gwen demanded, glaring up into his green eyes. "I'll give you evidence. I forced my dearest friend to labor long nights for the perfect gown so I'd be a credit to you. I endangered my acquaintance with the entire village to make sure every last detail of that assembly would be to your liking. I even scrubbed the floors of the market hall! Do you know how long I had to soak my hands in my mother's lotion afterward to soften them again?" She shook her gloved hands at him, and he flinched.

"All that," Gwen concluded, "just so my father could steal a few pieces of silver he could have snatched at any time and you wouldn't even have noticed!"

He gazed down at her, and one corner of his mouth turned up. "You provide an excellent defense."

"And why? You claim to be a man who likes to solve puzzles. This is the best solution you could find?"

He sighed. One hand brushed her shoulder, and she realized he was stroking back a strand of hair that had fallen. "I've had few who would stand by me, Gwen. I'm not used to trusting people."

Just as the squire had warned her. "London must be an awful place," she said, crossing her arms over her chest. "You are well rid of it."

He sighed. "Unfortunately, without those jewels, I have no choice but to return."

Oh, but he was determined to plunge a knife in

her heart. She would not think about him leaving now, not with her father starting to snore on the chair.

"As you said, we can discuss that tomorrow," she replied. "For now, I should collect my father and get him in bed. Does Mrs. Bentley have Dolly?"

He had been gazing at her father; now his look speared back to her. "Dolly?"

"Yes. She and my father's lantern were both missing when I returned home. He takes them both on his rounds. Remember how you and I met?"

"I will never forget." The soft cadence of his voice was like cool ointment on her heated emotions.

"But I haven't seen Dolly," he continued. "She wasn't in the butler's pantry. And Mrs. Bentley is apparently still helping at the assembly. I was lucky to catch Rob as he was returning."

Gwen seized his hand. "That's it, then! Don't you see? Find what's become of Dolly, and you may well solve this entire puzzle!"

Gwen's passion for her subject was always Trevor's undoing. He wanted to believe her. He couldn't believe how much it had hurt to think that all her attentions had been nothing but a ruse to keep him from scrutinizing her father's nefarious plans. She was obviously hurt he didn't completely trust her.

How could he? Nearly everyone who should

have cared for him—his father, his mother, people who claimed to be friends—had proven false. He'd spent much of his adult life tracking down servants, spouses and relatives who had betrayed their loved ones for money. With such evidence before him of the depth to which humanity could sink, it was all too easy to believe the worst of Gwen and her father, even when a part of him cried out that she must be innocent.

He straightened off the wall, and she stepped back from him. "Very well," he said. "Call Dolly."

But it was not so simple. Gwen called "Dolly, come!" and "Dolly, here!" and no massive beast bounded through the door. Gwen hurried into the entryway and tried again, but no paws thundered down the stairs. She shouted out the front door, and no booming bark echoed in response.

She turned to Trevor, eyes wide. "Where can she be?"

He knew panic when he saw it. She was as worried about her dog as she had been about her father, but then he supposed Dolly had been more reliable of late than Horace Allbridge. And he could still remember the fear that had stabbed at him when he'd thought someone had made off with Icarus.

He put an arm about Gwen's shoulders. "We'll find her. Would she leave the estate?"

Gwen leaned against his chest, and Trevor fought the urge to gather her closer. "No. She's trained to stay on the Blackcliff grounds unless she's with one of us. But she's also trained to come when I call. Something's wrong."

Trevor had to agree. Someone had invaded Black-cliff Hall that night, topping tables and moving valuables as if to steal them. If not Horace Allbridge, then who?

Mrs. Bentley certainly needed the money, but he could not believe her such a talented actress that she could be any less devoted than she seemed. Dorie seemed just as innocent, and with no connections outside Blackcliff, neither of them could have sold the pilfered silver easily. Besides, both Mrs. Bentley and Rob Winslow had been at the assembly. The only person besides Trevor who had the run of the house, knew the value of its belongings and had been missing from the assembly was Gwen's father, which put Trevor right back where he had started from.

He glanced up to find that lights were bobbing up the drive. The constable and Rob Winslow were on their way. Gwen must have seen them, as well, for she straightened away from him, leaving him chilled. "What will you do?"

He heard the worry in her voice. He'd made her doubt him even as he'd doubted her. Yet he had to think beyond the feelings she raised in him. He should err on the side of caution and put Horace Allbridge in jail, where he could neither steal nor injure himself or others in a drunken haze.

Forgive us our debts as we forgive our debtors.

The thought of the Bible verse came easily enough, but it wasn't in his nature to forgive. Forgiveness wouldn't earn him the respect of his peers. It didn't win him a place in Society. It couldn't pay for Blackcliff's upkeep or put food on its table. Yet as Rob drew up to the house with Mr. Casperson in tow, Trevor knew what he must do. Despite what anyone thought of him, he must act like an honorable gentleman if that was what he hoped to be.

"Thank you for coming, Casperson," he said, holding out his hand to the constable. The shopkeeper still wore his dark brown suit from the assembly, though his cravat was wilting, and the lower button on his striped waistcoat looked ready to pop off.

"Young Rob tells me you have a difficulty," Casperson said, rocking back to look up into Trevor's face.

"It seems someone broke into Blackcliff Hall while we were at your fine assembly," Trevor explained. "Mr. Allbridge was apparently discomposed attempting to stop the thief."

Casperson raised a bushy brow as if he could not believe the truth of that statement, but Rob Winslow was grinning at Trevor in approval. Better, Gwen gazed at him with worshipful eyes, a smile trembling on her lips. He felt as if the very air was fresher, warmer.

"Odd the miscreant decided on Blackcliff," Casperson rumbled, hands splayed across his belly as he eyed the house. "Not many would wish to take on Allbridge's Dolly."

"And that is part of the mystery, as well," Trevor agreed. "The mastiff is missing."

The constable pursed his fleshy lips and whistled. "Best I look around, then." He heaved himself up the stairs for the door.

Trevor leaned closer to Gwen. "I'll keep him busy. You and Rob take care of your father. As soon as we find Dolly, I'll bring her to you."

She clasped his hand, tears misting her eyes. "Thank you."

Trevor nodded, straightening. He felt as if he'd done the right thing, but how could he be sure?

Lord? The thought came unbidden, but Trevor forged ahead. *If You do listen to mere mortals, help me find out who's responsible for this trouble. And if You want me to forgive, You'll need to help me with that, too.* Feeling a little foolish for even asking, he followed the constable into the house.

Chapter Eighteen

While Trevor took Mr. Casperson to the butler's pantry, Gwen enlisted Rob's help to get her father down to the gatehouse and into bed. She'd tried questioning her father about that night, but he was too far gone with gin to make any sense.

"And you saw nothing, heard nothing strange when you returned from the assembly?" she pressed Rob as she escorted him to the door of the gatehouse.

He shook his head. "Not a thing. But I'm glad you were able to change Sir Trevor's mind about your father." He paused by the door, feet shuffling against the stone floor. "Though I expect you could change any man's mind, if you liked."

"I just explained the truth," Gwen protested. "Sir Trevor can be quite reasonable if you try."

Rob glanced up at her, dark eyes sad. "He won't stay, Gwen, you know that."

Gwen swallowed. "I know no such thing."

Rob's face tightened. "He's London-born—you can see that." He waved a large hand. "This place, all of us, we're nothing to him."

"We could be a great deal more," she insisted.

He dropped his hand. "I can see this ending one of two ways—he stays for your sake and comes to hate you because he's imprisoned here, or you go with him and come to hate him for taking you away from Blackcliff."

"Isn't there a third ending?" Gwen begged. "Couldn't we both stay and live happily ever after?"

"That's a tale for children, Gwen." He took up her hand and pressed it. The touch only made her all the more anxious for him to leave.

"We're not children anymore," he murmured. "You know what I feel for you. I was thinking about it as I went for Mr. Casperson. Perhaps I don't need to work at Blackcliff Hall. My father's getting on. I could take over the smithy. It's not a grand estate, but it's steady work, enough for me to support a wife."

She pulled her hand from his. "I'm glad for you, Rob. You'll make some woman a wonderful husband."

"But not you, eh?"

She shook her head, unable to say the words aloud that would wound him.

He nodded. "I thought that's the way the wind

blew. I'll not trouble you further. But know that if you need help, I'll be waiting."

"Thank you." It was all she could say. He nodded again and closed the door behind him.

Oh, but he had to be wrong! She leaned her back against the door and wrapped her arms about her now thoroughly wrinkled gown. She didn't understand why Trevor had blamed her father, why he hadn't turned that clever mind of his to some other answer when faced with tonight's puzzle. It hurt to think he had considered her part of some plot against Blackcliff.

Yet she still wanted him to stay. She still hoped he'd fallen in love with her. She still loved him.

Miracles happen, Father. Your Bible is proof of that. Work things out as only You can.

She wanted to return to the Hall to help Trevor and search for Dolly. But she couldn't leave her father. Even in this state he'd been known to wake with the oddest notions.

So, instead of returning to Trevor's side, she changed out of her finery. She carefully lay the dress between pieces of tissue in her clothes press, then donned one of her work gowns instead. Until Dolly was safely back in her kennel at the rear of the gatehouse, Gwen had no intention of climbing into bed.

Father, please protect them all—my father, Trevor, Dolly, Mr. Casperson, all who serve at

Blackcliff. Help us find the one who caused such trouble and bring him to justice.

Keeping one ear tuned for any movement up-stairs, she went to the kitchen and began pulling down the herbs and tonics that went into her gin cure. Mrs. Billings at the George Inn had given her a recipe she used for guests who imbibed too much and were sick in the morning. Gwen had improved upon it. She was shaking the corked bottle to mix the ingredients when she heard a sound at the back door. Setting down the vial and wiping her hands on her apron, she hurried to answer.

Trevor stood on the doorstep, leash in his gloved hands. Dolly bounded through the door, tongue lolling, taking him with her. Before he could pull her up, she bumped against the worktable, shaking Gwen's concoction.

"Sit!" Gwen commanded, and the mastiff plopped herself on her haunches and grinned.

Gwen bent to wrap her arms around Dolly's neck and bury her face in the cool hair. *Thank You, Lord!*

"She wasn't hurt," Trevor said.

Looking up, she found him watching her. His raven hair was ruffled as if the wind had wound through it, and his cheeks were pink with the cold.

She rose. "Thank you for bringing her home. Where did you find her?"

"Locked in the kitchen. Mrs. Bentley discovered her and your father's lantern when she returned from the assembly. But there's more."

Gwen frowned. "What?"

"Casperson found blood at the outer door to the butler's pantry, on the way to the kitchen."

"Blood?" Gwen's hand flew to her mouth. "Father!" She turned and ran for the stairs.

Her father was snoring, face up, on his bed when she dashed into the room. Gwen lit the lamp on the side table. He didn't look pale, lying on the wide old bed. No telltale stains spread across the wool blankets he'd pulled up to his chin.

A movement by the door caught her eye, and she saw that Trevor had followed her and was glancing around the little room.

"I put Dolly in her kennel," he said.

Gwen nodded, then bent over her father, fingers probing. He didn't turn, didn't jerk away as if she'd touched a tender spot. She pulled back the covers and glanced along his body.

"Nothing," she said with a breath of thanksgiving.

"Check his head," Trevor said. "The back to be precise."

Gwen slid her hand between her father's head and the thin pillow. His hair was matted with something thick and slimy, and a lump was rising at the back. He grunted in his sleep and turned away from her. She pulled away her hand and saw brick-red ooze on her fingers. "He hit his head!"

"If he had, the wound would more likely be on the front or one side," Trevor said as she hurried for the porcelain basin and pitcher on her father's washstand. "This looks more as if someone hit him."

Pitcher in her hand, Gwen sucked in a breath. "Who?" she demanded, glancing at Trevor.

In the dim light, his face looked guarded. "We don't know. Casperson is still searching the estate."

Gwen splashed water over her hand and into the basin, then seized up the hand towel and returned to her father's side. "Do you think it was the same person who's been moving the shepherd?" she asked, setting her tools on the table next to the lamp. The light sparkled on the water, blurring the image of the rose at the bottom of the basin.

"I think it highly likely."

She wet the towel and set about sponging the blood off her father's hair. He curled up tighter with a snort, but she wasn't about to stop until she learned more about his wound. "Well, at least we know it wasn't my father. He certainly didn't strike himself over the back of his head."

"No, but he might have had a compatriot who turned on him."

Gwen rolled her eyes, wringing the towel in the basin and turning the water pink. "Your mind jumps in the oddest directions. My father doesn't have many compatriots, you know."

He leaned against the doorjamb and crossed his arms over his chest. The movement swept his coat wider, making his shoulders look ever broader. "And why is that?"

"For one thing, he's the steward of Blackcliff. That puts a distance between him and others. For another, he's been a melancholy mess since my mother died." She wrung out the towel again.

"I would have thought the good people of Blackcliff would overlook such things."

She parted the wet hair and examined her father's skull. "Sarcasm does not become you, sir."

"You mistake me. I have been told, by reliable sources, that the people of Blackcliff are paragons. It seems to me those sources may be right. Yet now you tell me that they could not forgive your father for mourning his wife, and I find that someone was willing to behead the poor fellow to steal from the Hall. You cannot have it both ways, Gwen."

The wound was a jagged slash across the skin, but she didn't think it went deeper. "I suppose I can't," she murmured. He already thought the worst of her father. What harm in telling him the truth? She turned to Trevor.

"It was the drinking. He made a nuisance of himself in the village, alienated every friend he had. He even showed up at services once and vomited on Mr. Newton. It was horrible."

She shook herself to throw off the memory. "He blamed everyone for her loss—the colonel for refusing to give her a warmer place at the Hall when she was suffering, John Cord for not sneaking away more often to help us, Mr. Newton for not praying hard enough. For a time I think he even blamed me for not giving her the proper cures."

Trevor's face sagged as if he felt the pain with her. "Didn't he know you were grieving, too?"

Tears were starting, and she blinked them back. "He did, in time. He finally realized the damage he was causing when the colonel discharged him."

He straightened. "Your father was let go?"

She nodded. "Right before the colonel died. He told my father to leave Blackcliff and never return. But the colonel wanted me here, to help him with his imagined illnesses. I told him I'd only stay if my father could remain. So he let us continue living in the gatehouse. He must not have noted my father's discharge in the estate records, because when the solicitor came to look over the estate, he assumed my father was still steward."

Those green eyes were disappointed. "And you let me assume the same."

Guilt tugged at her. "Yes. But you needed him. No one else has his knowledge about Blackcliff."

"You realize, Gwen," he said with a sigh, "you've just given me another reason to suspect his hand in the mischief."

Gwen rose. "Then let me clear his name. Let me help you search for this person who assaulted him."

"No." His look brooked no argument. "It isn't safe."

"But you can't ask me to sit and watch the people I love get hurt." She moved closer, intent on making her case. "People here trust me. They're more likely to answer my questions than yours."

"That much is true," he agreed, begrudgingly, she thought. "But what if you find your father is involved?"

"He isn't," Gwen promised. "And it will be better for everyone if we learn the truth."

"Perhaps," he said, turning away. "But in my experience, not everyone appreciates the truth."

Chapter Nineteen

Gwen woke to her father's groan and brought the tonic to him straight away. He coughed and made a face as he handed the emptied cup back to her. "Vile concoction."

"Vile habit," she countered. "Now turn your head so I can get a good look at your bump."

"Bump?" He turned with a frown, and Gwen removed the bandage she'd put on before retiring. The swelling had gone down a little with no sign of fresh blood. *Thank You, Lord!*

"What do you remember of last night?" she asked, settling back beside him.

He tugged the covers closer. "Couldn't stop thinking about your mother. One cup led to two."

"Or six. I found the empty bottle before retiring."

He rubbed a hand against his grizzled chin. "Funny, that. I don't remember drinking so much. I was well enough to start my rounds."

"How did you end up in the butler's pantry?"

He frowned. "Butler's pantry? I didn't go into the house proper. I was coming around the kitchen when Dolly started pulling. I knew everyone was down at the assembly, so I thought I should discover what spooked her."

Gwen leaned forward. "What did you find?"

He dropped his hand and shrugged. "Don't remember. Things get hazy from there on. Sounds like I hit my head."

Small wonder Trevor suspected him with a story like that. "Sir Trevor found you passed out in the butler's pantry," Gwen informed him, straightening, "with the house tore up and the silver all around you."

Her father stiffened. "I'm no thief!"

"Well, someone wants us to think so!"

Her father's bloodshot eyes narrowed. "Is Sir Trevor of a similar mind?"

"He remains unconvinced of your innocence," Gwen said, rising. "You will need to beg him his forgiveness, and it wouldn't hurt to do the same for Rob Winslow."

Her father stuck out his lower lip. "A gentleman doesn't beg."

"An honorable gentleman doesn't neglect his duty. Or crawl into a gin bottle because he pities himself."

He raised his head. "Fine words to give your father."

"I wouldn't have needed to say them once. I intend to help Sir Trevor find the real troublemaker, Father, but I cannot help you save your job if you don't help yourself."

He collapsed sullenly against the headboard. "What do you want of me?"

"To begin with, I want you to pour every ounce of gin into the ground."

"Wasted money! What if we need it for medicinal purposes?"

"I have an entire cupboard of tonics."

"And no interest in making more."

Gwen leveled a finger at him. "Do not think to blame this on me, sir. I'm going to dress for services. If you intend to go with me, I suggest you do the same."

"Bossy little thing, aren't you?" he complained. But he threw back the covers and swung his legs off the bed. "Today you remind me too much of your mother."

"Good," Gwen said, heading for the door. "Then perhaps you'll listen to me for once."

Trevor had slept little. He could not like his behavior last night. He'd leaped to the conclusion that Allbridge was a villain, despite evidence that pointed to the man's innocence. It hadn't taken much thought to realize why. He'd felt betrayed. Allbridge had promised him the end of his trials, offering a fortune in jewels, and Trevor had latched onto the idea like a cripple to a crutch. That it might all be a story designed to keep him off guard drove him mad.

No one spoke of the matter at St. Martin's that morning. Trevor took his place in the Blackcliff pew to nods of greeting from his neighbors and a tremulous smile from Gwen. At least Casperson was no gossip. It seemed no one else knew about the trouble at Blackcliff last night.

As soon as Trevor returned to the Hall, however, he went looking for proof that the jewels existed. He read and reread the estate ledgers until the lines blurred and only succeeded in finding one discrepancy.

The year after the mine had closed, the expenses for the estate outpaced its income, yet the ledger balanced. Was that evidence that the colonel had used one of his jewels to pay the difference, as Allbridge had said, or simply an arithmetic error? It seemed a slim chance on which to pin his hopes.

Mrs. Bentley rapped on the open door of the library. "Excuse me, Sir Trevor, but Mr. Allbridge and Miss Allbridge would like to speak with you."

"Send them in," Trevor said, pushing the book away from him on the desk. That Gwen thought she needed to be announced told him that he wasn't the only one with misgivings about last night.

Gwen was hesitant when she entered, as well, hovering to one side of her father as he came forward. Even her brown-wool coat looked subdued.

Her father turned his hat in his gnarled hands, gray head hanging, as he apologized for his behavior. Gwen's gaze darted between him and Trevor as if she was trying to gauge the success of his performance.

"Sit down, Allbridge," Trevor said when her father wound to a stop. "I have some questions for you."

His steward perched on a chair before the desk. Trevor was certain Gwen would busy herself elsewhere in the room to eavesdrop as she always did, but instead she sat in a chair near her father as if to keep an eye on him. Trevor had seen more kindly looks on the faces of affronted tutors when he'd been hauled in for some infraction.

"He says he doesn't remember anything about last night," she told Trevor before he could question her father. "Dolly reacted to something in the kitchen. He went in to investigate and blacked out."

"I was hit," her father protested, bending and twisting his head so Trevor could see the lump.

"And you never saw your attacker?" Trevor pressed.

"No, sir," Allbridge said, straightening. "But I'd like to."

Trevor smiled grimly. "So would I."

"What did Mr. Casperson find?" Gwen put in. "Was anything actually stolen?"

"Not that we can determine. But I have another mystery for you, Allbridge." He turned the book so that it faced Gwen's father and pointed to the column. "What do you make of that?"

His steward rose and leaned over the book as if he thought Trevor meant to trap him. His blue eyes moved back and forth as he scanned down the page, then widened. "That's when he had me sell the ruby," he said, gaze rising to meet Trevor's.

Trevor leaned back in the chair. "You still insist the jewels exist? Last night you sounded as if it was all a story."

He waved a hand. "Last night I was in my cups!"

"Father, what is this?" Gwen asked. "You never told me about any jewels."

He kept his gaze on Trevor, as if trying to convince him. "I was sworn to secrecy. Besides, you were busy with your mother." He pointed to the page. "But this proves Umbrey had access to funds he didn't consider part of the estate."

Trevor wanted to bottle the man's confidence and drink it down. Before he could respond, however, Gwen spoke up.

"Who else knows?"

Her father turned to eye her. "No one, as far as I know."

She shook her head and rose to sweep up to the desk. "I think you're wrong. Someone else knows. He was here last night, and he's been here for weeks, searching. Last night he tried to blame it on you, Father. We have to find those jewels before he does!"

Trevor wasn't sure whether to groan or cheer. Gwen Allbridge was a force to be reckoned with, but he had a feeling she was taking on more than she knew.

"No one would argue with you on that score," he told her. "But your father and I have already searched the lower floors to no avail."

"Then we'll simply start with the upper," she replied, raising her head.

Horace Allbridge gave Trevor a glance that said he, too, thought they were both in trouble. "It's not so easy, girl."

She ignored him. "They can't be in an obvious place," she said, gaze on the ceiling as if she were trying to see through the plaster to where the jewels had been stashed. "He would have found them before now." Her gaze snapped down to Trevor's. "I know—we should question the staff!"

"Miss Allbridge," Trevor said and had the satisfaction of seeing her still. "I've conducted a few investigations. While I agree that questioning the staff is generally useful, no one on the staff has been here long enough to know anything about how the colonel chose to live. I'd suggest questioning someone who knew the man well."

She nodded eagerly. "John Cord! Of course! Surely he'd know where the colonel would hide his valuables. I've been meaning to bring him some of Mrs. Bentley's beef soup. That should give us an excellent reason to call."

She was heading for the door before Trevor could agree.

"Best you go with her," her father murmured, watching her. "Keep her out of trouble."

"Is that possible?" Trevor asked, but he rose and strode after her. If John Cord knew nothing of the jewels, Trevor still might learn something from him. And if he did know about the jewels, he could be dangerous.

With her bonnet on her head and her basket on her arm, Gwen set out with Trevor for John Cord's cottage at the opposite end of the village. "We won't mention the jewels," she promised as they left the grounds. "Just ask him some questions."

"Perhaps you could leave the questioning to me."

She cast him a glance. His greatcoat streamed behind him as he strode along, the hem whisking about his boots. She wasn't entirely sure of him this morning, but it seemed the attentive gentleman from last night was more in evidence. "I thought we agreed people trust me more."

"All the more reason for me to be seen as the difficult one."

She nodded. "Yes, I can see you in that role."

She meant to tease him, but he immediately sobered. "I must apologize for last night," he said as they reached the nearest edge of the village. "You obviously have a burden to bear. I should not have added to it."

His kindness fell over her like a warm blanket on a cold night. "I keep hoping nights like that are at an end," she said with a sigh. "I pray for him, a lot."

He was quiet a moment as they passed the George. Mrs. Billings was out sweeping the front step. Gwen raised a hand in greeting.

"Does God answer when you pray?"

She turned to him in surprise. "Of course! He answers you, doesn't He?"

He gazed off over the dark rooftops to where the fells rose purple in the distance. "Perhaps I haven't had as many opportunities to pray."

The more she knew of him, the more she suspected that his life had not been as privileged as she'd originally supposed. Yet even if he had been wealthy, surely he'd had petitions—illness, deaths of friends or family, loneliness. Had he never prayed about those?

"How did you pray when you were young?" she asked, taking his arm and steering him around a waiting wagon in front of Mr. Casperson's shop. "Mother always heard my prayers before bed and guided me if I strayed too far afield." And the memory no longer hurt as much as it had a few months ago.

"Which of these cottages belongs to Cord?" he asked.

"That one," Gwen said, pointing with her basket at the smallest of the group. She led him to it and only later realized he had never answered her question.

Unfortunately, their trip did little good. John Cord welcomed them nicely enough, as if eager for company, but he couldn't tell them much about the colonel's last days.

"A very ill man," he said in his slow voice as they sat in the main room of his cottage. The stone house held only two rooms, one for living and one for sleeping. A fireplace in the center managed to warm the place, but the soot on the ceiling told Gwen it did so badly. Dust flecked the worn floorboards, and the three chairs around the center table did not match. A shame the colonel had not seen fit to leave something to his former valet in his will as most masters did.

"The colonel truly wasn't ill," Gwen told Mr. Cord and Trevor, who dwarfed the spindly chair he'd been given. "I think he worried himself to death."

"He had a lot of fears at the end," Mr. Cord agreed, running his hands along his breeches. He cast Trevor a quick glance. "Living alone will do that to a man. He even set me loose, as if he knew he would shortly have no need for a valet."

"Perhaps he ran out of funds once the mine was closed," Trevor ventured, watching him.

John Cord coughed into his hand before answering. "I have wondered the same. He never paid me my last wages."

"We'll certainly see to that," Gwen promised.

"Very likely the matter is noted in the estate books," Trevor said smoothly. "Of course, the old fellow might have hidden the money."

"Not the colonel," Mr. Cord protested. "If he had anything of value, he kept it in sight. Look how he doted on that statue."

Trevor tried a few more questions, but the answers must not have satisfied him, for he quickly concluded the visit and bid the valet adieu. Gwen made sure to leave Mr. Cord the soup Mrs. Bentley had sent. Remembering his pride about charity, she waited until he was shaking Trevor's hand, then set it near the hearth where he'd find it after they'd gone.

As soon as they'd started back toward Blackcliff, however, she turned to Trevor. "You don't believe he wasn't paid. You think he's trying to steal your money."

"His pay was carefully noted in the estate books," he said with a certain stubbornness. "Your father saw to it. If anything, the man was overpaid. French valets with experience serving kings are paid less."

"But you can see he needs it," she tried. "He's ill. He cannot work."

"Then he should apply to the poorhouse."

Gwen frowned at him. "That isn't amusing."

"I didn't intend it to be. My point was that there are provisions to support the poor. He would be wise to make use of them instead of trying to take advantage of me."

Gwen stopped in the road. "My word! I'd never have taken you for a miser. Or it is that you dislike John Cord so much?"

He glanced back at her, but he kept walking. "He has given me no reason to like him."

Gwen hurried to catch up with him. "Are you still upset about Icarus? Or do you think he knows more about the jewels? You cannot expect him to volunteer information you don't request."

"Actually, I'm known for being rather good at learning information I didn't request. My skills seem to have floundered here at Blackcliff. I wonder why." He cast her a pointed look.

Gwen dimpled. "Now I know you're teasing. But don't fall into the dismals. I've thought of somewhere else the colonel might have kept his jewels."

That stopped him. "Indeed."

His brows were up, and sunlight glinted in his green eyes. "Indeed," she promised. "The mine."

He frowned. "But anyone might walk in and find them."

"Not at all. Wad is precious. When the mine was closed, the entrance was sealed with a padlocked door." She fished in her basket. "I have Father's keys."

He shook his head. "Do I want to know how you got those?"

"I'm certain you can hazard a guess after last night," she replied, face heating. "So, shall we try it?"

"Not without provisions," he said, but he started for Blackcliff just the same. "I want a lantern at the very least."

"We can find that at the gatehouse," Gwen replied. "Anything else?"

Trevor eyed her. "Yes. A brace of stout pistols, loaded and half-cocked. I don't know what we'll find at the mine, but I plan to be ready for it."

Chapter Twenty

Trevor wasn't sure what he had expected, but he found himself disappointed on his first sight of the fabled Blackcliff Mine. It consisted of a tunnel in the rocky side of the fell, with piles of silty black tailings surrounding the entrance. A thick slab of oak planking served as a door, locked with a stout iron padlock. Trevor put out a hand to stop Gwen as she selected the key from the ring.

"A moment, please." He crouched on the sharp gravel before the door and eyed the lock. Orange around the edges showed where snow and rain had rusted the device. He was more interested in the scratches marring its face.

"When was the last time this door was opened?" he asked, rising.

Gwen cocked her bonneted head. "Very likely when the colonel's solicitor came to inventory the estate before putting it up for sale. Father checks that the lock is in place once a month and opens the door quarterly to be sure no one has tampered with the place."

Trevor looked over the door. "Did he ever find signs of tampering?"

"No. We've been fortunate. Some of the other closed mines have been plagued by smugglers. They tunnel in from the sides or above and bypass the locks. Some of the mine owners post guards. Colonel Umbrey didn't feel that was necessary here. All the land connected to the Blackcliff Mine belongs to Blackcliff."

Trevor stepped aside. "Well, let's see if he was right."

She inserted the key, and the lock rasped open. Trevor seized the iron handle of the door and heaved.

Chill, stale air darted out as if glad to escape. He held his lantern high as he took a step inside. His boots crunched on rock. Rough walls rose on either side, pitted and scarred. Here and there, something glittered in the light.

"This is wad," Gwen said, scraping a bit of rock off the wall. It sparkled as she crumbled it in her fingers. "You can see it's fairly soft. It's not hard work to mine it."

"Yet here it sits, waiting." The idea frustrated him. Yard on glittering yard of the stuff, and without those jewels or some other source of investment, he couldn't touch it.

"Until we can repair the timbers," Gwen said as if reading his mind. "Mr. Dennings's death was a terrible tragedy. I know none of us want it repeated. But once the mine is repaired, you wait and see. Blackcliff will flourish then."

If there was anything left of Blackcliff. Trevor could not argue that the place needed repairs. The beams holding up the roof were cracked and bent. Water trickled down the walls beside him. Even closed up, the mine suffered from the cold of winter, the heat of summer. The very air tasted metallic.

"Is there a storeroom? Any place for a foreman?" he asked, moving a few feet deeper into the tunnel. The uneven walls disappeared beyond the light of his lantern. He could only hope the colonel's hiding place wasn't too deep, as he refused to risk Gwen's life, or his own.

"The wooden buildings were all at the entrance when the mine was operating," she replied, following him. "The colonel let the villagers take the wood to repair their outbuildings."

Generous fellow, Umbrey, with everyone but the person who would buy his estate and the servants he'd left behind. Trevor turned to Gwen. "Then where would he have hidden the jewels?"

"The emergency box." She moved past him for an alcove in the wall a little ways along. "It held water, a whistle and bandages in case of a cave-in. Mother devised the scheme."

"Why do I sense that you had a hand in it, as well?"

He could see her smile as she tugged an iron strongbox from its storage place. "Because you are a gentleman of uncommon good sense."

The light at the entrance flickered, as if something had passed across it. Trevor looked back in time to see the door swinging shut. The rush of air swept toward him along with the darkness and a resounding thud.

Gwen straightened, blinking. "What happened?"

Trevor bundled her into the alcove with the strongbox. "We have company. Stay here."

She immediately scrambled out again. "I will not! Give me that lantern. You need both your hands."

Much as it pained him to admit it, she was right. "At least stay behind me," he said, handing her the lantern and pulling out one of the pistols from his greatcoat. At the sight of the long barrel, she sobered and nodded agreement.

Trevor started for the door. In the still air, the only sounds were the drip of water down the wall and his footfalls on the rock.

A tiny sliver of light showed through the keyhole. Trevor bent and peered out but saw only the ground before the entrance. He could hear nothing through the thick oak. Straightening, he glanced at Gwen.

"Our visitor could be waiting, just outside. He's already proven he's not above hurting others. Let me go first. If there's any trouble, run for the Hall."

She shivered. "We should have brought Dolly."

"Agreed. Now promise me you'll run."

She met his gaze. "If there's nothing I can do to help, I'll find help."

That was not the answer he wanted, but he knew he should have expected it. "Good enough." He wasn't sure what possessed him, but he bent and pressed a kiss against the cool of her forehead inside her bonnet. "Be careful," he ordered, straightening.

She nodded, eyes wide, in shock at his kiss or concern for their safety, he couldn't know. He eased open the door and peered out.

The slope below lay as empty as when they'd climbed it, the muddy road trailing down to a corner of the estate. He could see the Hall to his right and the village to his left. Not even a bird soared in the sky. All was silent, as if waiting.

Trevor ventured into the open, keeping an eye out for any movement. On either side, the tailings stood dark sentinel. Scraggly trees struggled up here and there among the rocks. There was no place to hide.

"Everything all right?" Gwen asked, stepping out of the mine and blinking in the sunlight as she blew out the lantern.

A rock rolled down the slope and dropped at Trevor's feet. He whirled.

There were more of them, tumbling toward him, crashing down the slope. No time to find who had started them sliding.

"He's above us!" he shouted, uncocking the pistol

and hurling it aside lest it discharge by accident. As Gwen looked up with a cry, he jumped to her and pressed her back against the door. The lantern fell at her feet.

Dirt showered him, and rocks thudded down on all sides. The avalanche knocked his hat from his head, carried it off down the hillside. The rumble trembled up his legs; the dust clogged his lungs. He held Gwen close, sheltering her with his body. She clung to him without a whimper.

Please, Lord. Hear me this once. Keep her safe.

As quickly as it had begun, the avalanche ceased. The last rock landed with a bounce beside Trevor's dusty boot. Slowly he raised his head and straightened.

"Are you all right?" she asked.

He flexed his shoulders and winced. "Well enough. Stay here."

Cautiously, he moved back until he could see up the slope. Bushes lay crushed, trees toppled and limbs missing. Dust hung in the air, already drifting with the breeze. Nothing else moved.

"He seems to be gone," he reported. *Thank You, Lord.*

Gwen sprang away from the wall and hurried to meet him. She peeled off her glove and reached for his face, standing on the toes of her dusty boots. Her fingers were warm as they probed his forehead, sifted dirt from his hair. He wanted to lean into the touch, hold it closer, hold her closer.

She relaxed onto her soles and held up her hand for his inspection. "No blood. That's good."

Not good enough. He had to get her safely back to the house. Their visitor could be anywhere on the mountain, above or below them, waiting. If he was willing to see them crushed in a rock slide, Trevor didn't want to know what else he'd try.

He kicked a rock aside on his way to the door. "Can you carry that strongbox?"

She made a face. "Doubtful."

Trevor sighed. "We can't leave it. This fellow is everywhere, and it wouldn't surprise me if he had a set of keys."

She opened her mouth as if to protest, but Trevor pulled out the other pistol. "I believe you know how to use this. You pointed it at me the night we met."

"I remember," she said, accepting the gun gingerly from him. "And if I haven't apologized before, I'm very sorry for ever considering you a thief."

"The feeling is mutual." In fact, his feelings since then had changed so much they astounded him. He bent to retrieve the lantern. Though the glass had broken, the candle remained intact. He pulled out his tinderbox and set about relighting it. "Keep a sharp watch and a ready gun," he said, gazing into the dark mine. "I'll be back with the box."

Gwen waited outside the mine. Dust settled around her, and she saw nothing else moving on the slope. The gun wavered just the slightest in her grip; she forced her hand to steady. She'd be no help to Trevor if she fell to pieces now.

Yet thoughts tumbled through her mind like the rocks that had pelted moments ago. Who had followed them to the mine? Why would he try to hurt them? Was he truly after the jewels? Were they in the mine, after all?

Why had Trevor kissed her?

Lord, thank You for keeping us safe, but help me focus!

Footsteps sounded, and she flinched, then realized it was Trevor returning. He had the box up on one shoulder. Handing her the lantern, he took back the pistol. Gwen relaxed as it left her hand.

"Lock it," he said with a nod toward the door. His gaze moved over the hillside, watchful. Gwen hurried to lock the door. As she returned to his side, he motioned her ahead of him with the pistol, steadying the box with his other hand. Gwen blew out the lantern and started down the slope, pausing only long enough to pull the other pistol from the rocks and hand it to Trevor.

As they continued down the hillside, she glanced back once in a while, but the only person she saw was Trevor. His hair was coated with dust; his greatcoat looked more gray than black. His face was just as grim.

Please, Lord, let that box be filled with jewels!

"I have some ointment for those scratches," she

offered, looking back. "I'll fetch it up to the house straightaway."

A smile teased one corner of his mouth. "Ah, so you don't care to see what's in this box."

"Of course I do!" Gwen smiled as she faced forward once more. "I meant straightaway, after you open it."

He chuckled. "Curious little thing, aren't you?"

"Well, we risked our lives to fetch it. We might as well see what we won."

"Agreed. I imagine your father would like to see what's inside, as well."

Gwen thought so, too, but her father wasn't in evidence when they reached the house and Trevor set down the strongbox inside the door. Mrs. Bentley and Dorie, who were tidying the withdrawing room, hadn't seen him, either. Gwen could only hope he'd gone home to sleep off the remaining effects from last night.

"What happened?" Mrs. Bentley cried when she'd gotten a good look at the two of them. "I've never seen anyone so dirty! Did you fall in a pit?"

Trevor pulled off his greatcoat as Gwen untied her bonnet. Even with her safe in Trevor's arms, the headpiece was covered in dust. Mrs. Bentley took it and his coat, clucking, and carried them off to be cleaned.

Trevor lifted the strongbox and started for the library. Gwen followed. Once inside the room, he laid it on the desk.

"Ready?" he asked, eyeing Gwen across the space.

She clasped her hands together and nodded, biting her lip to keep her emotions inside.

Trevor looked just as excited as she felt as he threw back the lid. But one look inside and he puffed out a sigh.

"A bladder of water, bandages, candles and a tinderbox," Gwen said, sorting through each item. "Oh, and here's the whistle."

"Marvelous." He strode to the window and stared out, back to her. He obviously didn't want her to see the disappointment on his face, but she found it in the sag of his shoulders.

She crossed to his side and put a hand on his arm. "Don't lose hope. We have plenty more places to look. You said yourself you hadn't tried the upper floors of the house, and there's the stable and the outbuildings and…"

"Gwen." The tone stopped her. He turned to gaze down at her. "I don't want you to search anymore."

She blinked. "You're giving up?"

He shook his head. "You mistake me. I will keep looking. I want you out of it."

She stepped back, raising her head. "I thought I did rather well today. You needed more than two hands at the mine."

He gathered both her hands in his and cradled them against his coat as if they were somehow precious to him. "You were brilliant—brave, clever, a true partner."

His words warmed her, but she could see he had made up his mind. "Then what?" she asked. "If I can be of such use to you, why won't you let me help?"

He gazed down at her a moment, face tight. "I don't want you to get hurt."

She smiled up at him, relishing the feel of his hands on hers. "I won't get hurt. I have you to protect me."

Instead of reassuring him, her statement only made his face tighten more. He pulled her close, until her head rested on his chest and his arms enfolded her. Gwen closed her eyes and leaned into the embrace, letting his touch fill her.

"And what if that's not enough?" he murmured. "I prayed today, Gwen. I prayed for your safety, and the Lord answered me."

Gwen leaned back to look up at him. "You see? I told you He answers prayer."

"And I have a feeling He expects us not to put ourselves in a position where we need Him to answer again," he returned.

Gwen sighed, allowing herself the luxury of one more moment in his arms. "I'm sure you're right. But when I see something that needs doing, I can't sit idly by."

"Even if others are capable of solving the problem?"

How could she answer? She could not claim her father incapable without risking his position. And, despite last night, she was certain he was getting better by the day. As for Trevor, well, she thought very little was beyond his skill.

She had fallen into the role of managing Blackcliff, first for Colonel Umbrey and then for her father. With her mother gone, she felt as if she'd taken on the burden for the entire village, as well. And many days, that burden felt far too heavy for her to carry alone.

But was she willing to set that burden on Trevor's shoulders instead?

Chapter Twenty-One

Trevor gazed down at Gwen. She'd become strangely quiet. Did she understand his concerns? For a moment, at the mine, he'd felt as if he couldn't breathe. It was one thing to put his life in jeopardy. Given his up-bringing, he had never been completely safe. Danger, of one kind or another, had followed him through school and onto the streets of London. He knew how to handle it, how to prepare for it, how to meet and defeat it. Nothing had prepared him for the fear that had assailed him at the thought of losing Gwen.

"So you'll stay out of it," he tried. "We're agreed that from here on, I search alone."

She peered closer, and he schooled his face to show only a polite smile. She sighed. "You're doing it again—putting on a mask that hides your feelings. Have I so offended you by wanting to help?"

He'd hidden behind a mask for years. Odd that

she was the only one who'd ever noticed. "You haven't offended me, Gwen. Just leave it be."

"I probably should," she said, slipping out his arms at last. "But this is so important. I know a fortune in jewels likely means little to a gentleman like you, but it means the world to me and my father."

A laugh forced its way out of him. "It means the world to me, too, I assure you. And I am no gentleman, Gwen. Perhaps it's time you learned the truth about the new master of Blackcliff."

Gwen took another step back so she could see all of Trevor. His face looked weary, his shoulders tense as if they carried a weight too great even for him. "I don't understand," she said.

"Very few do. I have done my best to make sure of it." He raised his chin as if making a decision. "I'm illegitimate, Gwen. My mother was an actress at the Theatre Royal in London. She wasn't very good on stage, but she excelled at getting gentlemen to fall in love with her. She was a great deal older than you when she ensnared a young naval midshipman who was related to the royal family. I was the result."

The picture was so far removed from the family she knew and loved that she could not grasp it. "But she must have loved him," she protested.

His gaze was pitiless, as if he'd resigned himself to this sordid truth long ago. "She was always devoted to the men who surrounded her, but her heart went to the highest bidder."

She refused to see his mother as so calloused. She'd raised Trevor, hadn't she? And he was one of the most honorable men Gwen knew. "Perhaps it was her way of providing for you."

He shook his head. "I admire how you can see the best in people, Gwen. But even my mother wouldn't agree with your assessment. She made my place in her life very clear. I was only of use as a source of income. My father's family provided her an allowance to clothe and feed me, you see. They also paid for my schooling. When I had finished school and the payments ended, she showed me the door."

"But she was your mother!" Gwen felt her face twisting in frustration.

He sighed. "She is, foremost, a survivor. She lives on her beauty, her ability to appear ageless. Sirens don't have grown sons. I am allowed to visit, when I let her know in advance and I use the kitchen door. I like to think she has a small fondness for me."

It hurt just hearing his story. "And your father? His family? Aren't they proud of the man you've become?"

"They do not acknowledge me publicly. However, they have let it be known that I am expected to do nothing to shame them. In all ways but name, they expect me to be a gentleman."

She swallowed. "You deserved better."

He stared at her, and she saw a light spring to his

eyes for a moment, as if she had offered him hope. Then he cast his gaze down to the strongbox lying open on the desk.

"Did I? I wonder. Sometimes I let the bitterness gain the upper hand. At school, I tried to cultivate an air of mystery, of detachment, but the rumors always spread."

"They judged you?"

She must have sounded as incensed as she felt, for she thought one corner of his mouth turned up. "Boys always look for someone to harass. Luckily, I was large enough and fast enough and fierce enough that few tried more than once."

She could imagine him backed against a wall, giving better than he got. "I would think that would win their respect."

"Some. Make no mistake, good men like Squire Lockhart offered me their friendship. Unfortunately, none of them was in a position to offer me a place as personal secretary or steward, and like John Cord, I refused to take charity. Instead, I found a way to make a living. I used my mother's connections to uncover the sins of my betters, then helped them hush those who would profit from that knowledge."

"What do you mean?" Gwen asked. "Are these the investigations you talked about?"

His gaze rose to meet hers, wearily. "Yes. The only pride I take in them is that I solved the puzzle. Uncovering embezzlement, blackmail, adultery, they are not something that endears you to the ones you help."

"I imagine not." And she could also understand why he had jumped so easily to the conclusion that her father must be his enemy. He'd probably seen any number of betrayals, and from people closer than a trusted steward.

"One of those I helped was my father," he continued. "I suppose I expected him to thank me, to finally acknowledge me. Instead, he arranged a baronetcy for me and sent me to the farthest part of England to an estate I cannot hope to redeem." He came around the desk and took her hands. "Those jewels are my one chance, Gwen. They will allow me to finally become the man I was meant to be."

"You are already that man," she said softly.

He snorted. "You think so? Although I had Bible classes in school, I never read the Bible until you handed it to me. My bedtime stories were sordid whispers down darkened corridors. I came here thinking only what Blackcliff could do for me, not what I could do for the people of Blackcliff."

"But you have helped!" When he rolled his eyes, she pulled him closer. "You have! You did not protest David Newton keeping his position. You gave Mrs. Bentley a place to live. You offered my father mercy."

"Because of you! You taught me how to see this place, these people. You taught me to care about their concerns." He let go of her hands to seize her shoulders. "Don't you see, Gwen? You've helped me become an honorable gentleman. I can't allow you to be hurt. Don't ask it of me."

Gwen laid her hand over one of his. "Very well. I'll stay out of it if it eases your mind."

His sigh was deep enough she felt it move through him. "Thank you."

She lifted her gaze to his. "But you are wrong, Trevor. If I have encouraged you to act honorably, I'm glad. But I don't believe you can make something from nothing. You are a gentleman at heart. You've proved that through your actions."

"Darling Gwen," he said softly. "Ever the optimist."

She wrinkled her nose. "If you don't believe me, ask God. He knows what He made you to be. The Bible says He knows us before we are born."

"And He chose this life for me?" His look spoke volumes. "Such kindness."

"Would you rather He let you die in the womb? Or sent you to no school at all and left you to fend for yourself on the street?"

"I would rather he had me born into a family."

Gwen hugged him close. "Oh, but you were born into a family, Trevor! You just didn't know it until you arrived in Blackcliff!"

Gwen was determined to keep her promise, no matter how difficult it was to refrain from offering suggestions or following Trevor about. She managed to convince him to let her find her father. At least one Allbridge might be of assistance!

But her father wasn't in the gatehouse when she went down to check. Nor could she find him in the stables with Rob or the kitchen with Mrs. Bentley. She was standing on the Blackcliff front step, hands on hips, wondering where else to check for him, when she spotted his lean figure loping from the back of the estate. Why was he out now, and without Dolly at his side?

Perhaps it was her conversation with Trevor, but a suspicion tickled the back of her mind. Surely he hadn't followed them to John Cord's cottage and then to the mine. Could he have started the avalanche accidentally? Then why not come to their aid afterward?

And why would he need to follow them? He had only to ask her, and she'd tell him everything she'd learned.

Gwen shook herself. No, her father must have some other reason for wandering about the estate. And she fully intended to find out what it was.

Unfortunately, he managed to evade her at the gatehouse, and when she returned to the manor later in the day, Mrs. Bentley reported that he had closeted himself with Trevor in the library. It seemed her father had located some early plans for the house as well as the plans for remodeling, and he and Trevor were comparing the two for any signs of hidden rooms or storage places. She was afraid they just might start taking axes to the walls. She could only hope the polished oak paneling would give them pause.

"And what did you determine?" she asked her father when she finally caught up with him at the Hall and returned with him to the gatehouse that evening for dinner.

"Ah, and you aren't supposed to be asking," he said, helping himself to a thick slice of the meat pie Gwen had baked. "Sir Trevor tells me that you've promised to leave the searching to him."

"So I did," Gwen said primly, watching him bring a forkful to his mouth. The fire popped in the grate beside them, and she could hear rain dripping from the trees outside. "But checking after you isn't part of that promise. What did you do while we were questioning Mr. Cord?"

"Me?" His gray brows went up, and he leveled his empty fork at her. "Now see here, miss. You have no call to be questioning your own father."

"And if I don't, who will?"

He snorted and dug back into his pie. "If you must know, I went to the kitchen and apologized to Mrs. Bentley. She had to do the cleaning up after my fall. Didn't seem right."

"That was good of you," Gwen replied, fork flaking off pieces of the golden crust. "Father, have I shamed you?"

"What?" His fork clattered to the plate. "Never! Who put such a thought in your head?"

Gwen laid her own fork aside. "I realized today that I've become a bit of a tyrant."

Her father chuckled. "That's God's truth."

"Well, you needn't agree so easily!"

He chuckled again. "Never been one to lie to my girl. You'd see right through me anyway." He sobered. "And you've had cause to take on more than your share, but that's going to change. I talked with Mr. Newton. He's going to help me get over my loss."

"Oh, Father, I'm so glad!" Gwen lay her hand over his. It was more frail than she remembered, but she thought she felt the strength inside. With the Lord's help, and David Newton's, she was certain her father would find that strength again, too.

He was up and out to the Hall early the next morning. Gwen thought about following, but she knew she'd only end up sitting around and waiting. That would drive her mad! Besides, a task had been given to her, one she'd been neglecting. She'd been afraid of taking her mother's place, of being less than her mother had been to the village. She'd tried to make everything perfect, when no one expected perfection except her.

Only You are perfect, Lord. Help me remember that and not demand it of myself or others.

She spent an hour out with Dolly gathering what she needed from the overgrown garden. Then she returned to the kitchen, cinched on her apron and opened her mother's recipe book. Memories assailed her—her mother writing, talking to Gwen all the while about steaming and shaking and everything else that had to be done to make the horehound syrup just right. Gwen swore she smelled the plant cooking long before she put it in the pot.

"People need this," she told Dolly, who was lying on the stone floor of the kitchen, watching Gwen as if hoping something juicy might drop. "I need this. It's like Mother is still here with me, and it's time I remembered that."

Two hours later, the horehound syrup sat cooling in vials about the room. The light gleamed on the pearly liquid, and she couldn't feel sad. She knew her mother would be pleased that Gwen had carried on her work, and she felt as if her heavenly Father was pleased, as well.

As soon as the bottles had cooled, she set two in her basket and started with Dolly for the village. One bottle went to Mrs. Wheaton, who reported that young Tim was doing better. Gwen promised to stop by later in the week.

The second was for John Cord. To Gwen's surprise, Dolly's growl rumbled out the moment the man opened the door.

"Miss Dolly," he chided, clearly hurt.

Dolly's hackles rose, and she bared her teeth.

"Dolly! Down!" Gwen ordered. The mastiff sank silently onto the ground, but her gaze never left the valet's haggard face.

"Is something wrong, Mr. Cord?" Gwen asked. "Have you had a stranger visit recently?"

He rubbed absently at the hip of his brown breeches. "As a matter of fact, I have. A gentleman by the name of Hunter was here only yesterday, just after you left."

"A gentleman of middling height, wearing a dark cloak?" Gwen asked eagerly.

"Yes, indeed. Do you know him?"

She was afraid she did. "He may be the man who's been sneaking about the Hall. What did he want from you?"

"He had a great many questions about the colonel. I believe they knew each other in India."

Of course! That's how he knew about the jewels.

"He sent me a note just a bit ago," the valet continued thoughtfully, tugging down at the ends of his elegant coat. "I was about to open it when I heard your knock. Would you like to see it?"

Would she! Gwen started to nod, then hesitated. She'd promised Trevor not to get involved. She should return to the Hall, let him come question the valet. But why waste all that time? If Mr. Hunter was sending notes, he might be staying as close as the George! How much better to learn what he wanted and then report to Trevor! Surely that was only reasonable.

"Yes, please," Gwen said. She motioned to Dolly. "Dolly stay!" Then she followed the valet into his cottage.

He shut the door behind her. "Will she stay there until you let her up?"

"Yes," Gwen replied, moving into the room. "She's very good that way."

The cottage looked much the same as when she'd seen it yesterday: worn, tired, much like its owner. The only difference was a scuffed portmanteau sitting near the door to the bedchamber.

"Are you traveling, Mr. Cord?" she asked, setting her basket on the table.

"I have hopes." He paused to cough, then went to a cupboard near the hearth and opened a drawer. "Now, where did I put that note?"

Gwen glanced around. If he had been meaning to read the note, as he'd said, it ought to be in plain sight. Yet the table had been empty until she'd set her basket on it.

He toddled back to her with a cloth over one hand. Before she knew his intention, he yanked it aside to reveal a long hunting knife. The blade gleamed even in the dim light.

"Be a good girl now," he said with a smile. "I just need your help to gain those jewels."

Chapter Twenty-Two

Trevor tapped the walls in his bedchamber, listening. A deeper noise might signal a hollow; a sharper noise a hidden safe. A shame the entire house was swathed in oak paneling; he would have spotted any irregularities a lot easier otherwise.

He and Allbridge had reviewed the plans for the house, which suggested few possibilities for hiding places. Compounding the problem was the fact that the colonel's renovations were impossible to reconcile. Trevor had agreed to send Gwen's father into Carlisle to consult with the architect who had supervised the work as well as the jeweler who'd accepted the ruby. His steward was down at the gatehouse packing for the trip.

Trevor hadn't seen anything of Gwen that day, but then he'd seen little of her since his confession in the library after the mishap at the mine. He'd come across her in the corridor yesterday evening when she'd come to collect her father for dinner. Her smile had been warm, and she'd reached out and squeezed his hand as if for encouragement.

He had had no idea a touch could be so significant. He wanted to stand taller, work harder, be a better person. Though he'd told her about his past, shared his doubts, still she made it clear that she admired him. It was humbling.

He'd had an even harder time believing that God could admire him, as well. The Bible certainly backed up her belief that God knew him personally; he'd read a verse to that effect only that morning in Psalms. But the Bible also showed a God who could only be pushed so far. He was the first to admit he'd sinned. Was he beyond redemption?

Yet a verse jumped to his mind instantly. *I came to seek and save what is lost.*

He clung to the thought as he continued rapping. He was so intent on his work that Mrs. Bentley had to clear her throat twice to get his attention.

"I beg your pardon, Sir Trevor," she said, venturing into the room with her white-haired head cocked as if she couldn't understand why the master had his ear to the wall. "I just returned from Mr. Casperson's and found this tacked to the kitchen door."

He took the sealed parchment from her hand. The blob of wax had been pressed in a half-moon seal, as if someone had stuck a spoon in it.

"Thank you, Mrs. Bentley," he said, breaking the seal.

She stood on tiptoe to see over the top of the letter. "Shall I wait for your reply?"

Trevor smiled at her as he glanced down at the words. "Very likely it's merely Mr. Newton or his sister inviting me to tea."

She dropped back onto the soles of her shoes, dark skirts rustling. "Oh, how kind of them."

Trevor began reading, and the air left his lungs in a rush.

"Sir Trevor?" his housekeeper ventured. "Is everything all right? You don't look at all well."

"I'm fine," Trevor lied. "But tell Rob to saddle my horse."

"Right away, sir." She hurried from the room.

Trevor glanced down at the note again and wasn't surprised to find his hand shaking. Gwen, kidnapped? And the ransom was the jewels or her life was forfeit. Oh, he was shaking all right, with anger.

How dare the villain threaten the woman Trevor loved!

He didn't question the feeling. It had been stealing over him for days. Her competence, her boundless energy, her faith and beauty were more than he could have dreamed. He'd thought he needed a wealthy, sophisticated wife to achieve his heart's desire, when what his heart craved was the love, the admiration and the family Gwen offered.

Now their future together was threatened by this unknown assailant, this coward who hid behind darkness, this cur who attacked old men and innocent women. He expected Trevor to cower, as well, to act like a gentleman and hand over the fortune, praying for his lady's safety.

Trevor may have learned to be a gentleman, but he didn't cower. He started for the door, then stopped.

The most important thing was Gwen's safety, and he thought he finally understood who was responsible for that. He went down on one knee and bowed his head.

Lord, I am learning who You are and how You want me to live. I've made many mistakes. The worst was blaming You for how others treated me. You've given me skills. You've made me strong. Help me become the man You want me to be. Help me be the man Gwen Allbridge needs, now and in the years to come. I pledge myself, such as I am, to You.

Determination filled him as he rose, and he knew he had made the right choice. He strode out the door.

He could not know who had Gwen or where she was being held. He had to look like the worried gentleman in case he was being watched. In Blackcliff, he was certain, worried gentlemen went to one place for solace—the church.

Ruth Newton answered his knock. "Oh, Sir Trevor." Her hand went to her hair as if she ever had a strand out of place, then brushed a wrinkle from the skirt of her fashionable spruce-colored gown. "We weren't expecting you."

Trevor was immediately on the alert, but he knew

better than to show it. "Forgive the interruption, Miss Newton. Have you seen Miss Allbridge recently?"

He watched for any sign of guilt, which he was certain would show easily on the woman's expressive face.

But Ruth Newton merely smiled fondly. "Not today, but I heard from Mrs. Wheaton that Miss Allbridge and Dolly were delivering a new batch of the horehound syrup, and I consider that a very good sign."

He wasn't sure why she was so pleased Gwen had made the syrup, but at least he knew Gwen had had Dolly with her. If Dolly was at Gwen's side, he could think of only two ways the villain had abducted Gwen—either the mastiff was dead or the abductor was someone Gwen and Dolly knew well. He prayed for the latter, for if Dolly was dead, he had far less hope for Gwen. And that thought nearly drove him mad.

"Do you happen to know where she went after that?" he asked.

Ruth frowned thoughtfully. "I haven't heard, but I would imagine she would take a bottle to dear Mr. Cord."

John Cord. He knew Gwen and Dolly well enough that he could have surprised them. He hadn't mentioned the jewels when Trevor and Gwen had visited, but he could easily have known of them. And Trevor had wondered from the first whether he was Blackcliff's mysterious visitor. Surely as the trusted valet he'd had a set of keys. And Trevor didn't recall seeing him at the assembly.

"Is your brother home?" he asked.

Ruth shook her head. "I'm so sorry, Sir Trevor, but no. He's out making calls."

Trevor leaned closer, and her blush deepened even as her gaze darted away from his. "Then I must ask you a favor," he murmured. "I need you to find a lad to hold Icarus for me."

She glanced up and quickly away. "Icarus?"

"My horse. It's very important that he be seen in front of the vicarage. If anyone asks after me, say only that I'm praying in the chapel and cannot be disturbed."

Her face puckered as she met his gaze. "Sir Trevor! What's happened that you must devote yourself to prayer?"

Dare he take her into his confidence? She seemed to truly care about Gwen.

"Miss Allbridge is in danger," he said. "I need people to think I'm here so I am free to act. If you would take care of my horse, I'd be in your debt."

He waited for her protest, not a little concerned she'd faint outright. But Ruth Newton raised her head, and her gray eyes narrowed. "Go into the chapel. There's a door to the left of the altar, half-hidden by the curve of the stone. It lets out into the orchard. No one will see you."

Trevor raised a brow. "You've a genius for subterfuge, Miss Newton."

"I protect what is mine, Sir Trevor," she replied, and he thought Joan of Arc must have looked just as fervent. She put a hand on his shoulder. "May God go with you, sir. I will pray for your safety, and Gwen's."

Gwen shook a copper-colored curl out of her eyes and frowned down at the ropes that bound her wrists to the sturdy arms of the hard-backed chair. She'd tried to outrun John Cord to the door, but he was surprisingly strong for an ill man. Perhaps it was his desperation.

He'd knocked her flat and kept the knife at her throat as he'd helped her up and walked her back to the chair. Now the remains of her bonnet, squashed in her struggles, lay crumpled in her lap. She was tempted to call for Dolly, but she didn't see how even the mastiff could make her way through that door.

"Why are you doing this?" she demanded, straining against the bonds.

Completely unconcerned with her plight, John Cord wandered out of the bedchamber. He wore the dark cloak she knew had been seen too many times at Blackcliff, his face hidden in the hood. His portmanteau was in one hand.

"Because I must have those jewels," he said, moving past her. "I'm going to meet Sir Trevor at the mine and get them now. As soon as I reach Bristol, I'll send him word where to find you."

He turned to her, and she saw his pale face was smiling. "It should only be a day or two. You will likely live to tell the tale, once I'm safely away."

He couldn't know that Trevor didn't have the jewels. What would he do when he found out? Would he hurt Trevor? Hurt Dolly? Hurt her? She had to distract him until she could think of a way to stop him.

"If you knew about the jewels," she pressed, "why didn't you just take them?"

His face twisted. "Because I never knew where they were kept. The colonel refused to tell me the location, even at the end when I begged him for my life. After all I'd done for him, all my years of faithful service in that heathen country, could he have spared just one to see me to a warmer climate? No!"

"Perhaps he didn't know you were sick," Gwen said. Was she mad to think the rope on her right felt looser? She pushed it upward for all she was worth, feeling it pinch through her gown.

"He knew. He sacked me to keep me from passing it along to him. But he didn't think to take my keys. I was able to slip into the house as often as I liked. I saw you nursing him. You're a kind girl. But he didn't tell you about the jewels, did he?"

Gwen shook her head. Yes, her right wrist was at least an inch higher than it had been. She relaxed for a moment, then renewed the pressure. "I never knew the story until my father told me a few days ago."

"And I wager he had to guess at that." John Cord paused to cough into his fist. "Oh, how I missed your mother's syrup. It was the only thing that quieted this cough."

"I have more," Gwen offered, hoping to distract him, but he was already moving again.

"The colonel couldn't care," he grumbled, slipping an apple into his pocket. "He was so close-mouthed. He died before he would tell me the jewels' location, even when I held this knife to his throat."

Gwen's wrist fell limp. "You killed him!"

"He was an old man," Cord snapped. "He died. And he told me nothing! And you and your father and that solicitor were so busy at first I couldn't get back into the Hall. And then your beloved showed up."

"Beloved?" *Think, Gwen! How can you escape?* She planted her feet against the stone floor and pushed. Could she stand and carry the chair with her?

He smiled slyly. "You didn't think I'd notice? You set your cap for the master the moment he arrived. Smart girl. Unless I miss my guess, he'll offer for you soon."

That set her blood to moving. An offer of marriage from Trevor? Oh, how she'd wanted that! But after his story yesterday, she wasn't sure she was the woman for him. He needed a wife who would bring credit to him, who would allow him to hold his head high. How could the imperfect daughter of his steward ever be that woman?

Please, Lord, help me! Show me how to escape. Protect Trevor and help him know the path he must take. If it leads him to me or away from me, Thy will be done.

As if he'd seen her moving, the valet came up to her and tugged on her bonds, humming to himself. "I thought he might have guessed my part in all this yesterday. That's why I followed you. I didn't mean to start that rock slide. I only wanted to scare you. Just like when I moved that statue."

"Please, Mr. Cord," she pleaded. "You can't leave me like this. Tell Sir Trevor you need money to go away. I'm sure he'll give it to you."

"He wouldn't even pay me my wages," he said with a sneer. He turned toward the back of the cottage, where a rear door led out onto a small garden, she knew. "I wish you luck, Miss Allbridge. I fear you'll need it. As for me, I cannot wait to kick the dust of Blackcliff off my feet."

He opened the door.

Trevor stood waiting, Dolly at his side.

"Good afternoon, Cord," he said. "I believe you have someone I love."

Chapter Twenty-Three

Trevor had no idea that a man of John Cord's condition or age could move that fast. One moment he was standing in the doorway, mouth agape, hand on the latch, and the next, cloak flaring behind him, he had scampered back behind a chair.

A chair that held Gwen.

Relief to see her alive rushed over Trevor, only to be followed by a wave of anger when he realized she was bound to her seat. Dolly trembled beside him, her growl reverberating up Trevor's arm.

"Back!" Cord warned. "Stay back, you and that monster. I warn you!" Gwen flinched to one side, and Trevor saw the glint of a knife in the man's hand.

Trevor's pulse pounded in his ears. "Let her go."

"Oh, I will, I will," the valet chattered between coughs that spattered Gwen's face with spittle. "As soon as you hand over the jewels and I'm safely on my way."

If the knife didn't touch her, his illness might. Trevor edged closer, gauging the distance between Dolly and the valet. Dolly's bark boomed, and Cord jerked back. Gwen's cry cut as sharp as the knife.

"Keep that monster back, I tell you," Cord demanded. "Tell her to lie down and be still." He pressed the knife against Gwen's throat, and Trevor froze.

This time Gwen didn't flinch. She met Trevor's gaze for a moment. Her face was calm, though he thought fear flickered in her dark eyes. "Quiet!" she ordered Dolly. "Down!"

With a huff of protest, Dolly sank to the floor beside Trevor.

"Much better," Cord said, withdrawing the blade a little. "Now, Sir Trevor, if you'd be so good as to hand over the jewels."

That he could not do, and he feared how the valet would react. "There are no jewels," Trevor said, watching Cord. "It was all a lie."

"What!" Cord's cough shook him and the knife, and this time Trevor flinched. "No! You're the one lying!"

Trevor took another step, readied himself to dive at the man the moment he had an opportunity. "I'm afraid not. Umbrey must have taken them with him to his grave."

"The wretch! It would be just like him!" Spittle flecking his lips, John doubled, hacking. Trevor leaped to his side and seized the hand that held the knife, forcing it away from Gwen. The valet twisted in his grip, screaming curses. Trevor ignored him, intent on only one thing—getting the knife as far from Gwen as possible. He shoved his elbow into the valet's gut and the knife fell, clattering against the stone floor.

Once again relief was profound, but Trevor must have relaxed his grip, because Cord slipped away, stumbling backward. Trevor put himself between the man and Gwen. "Enough! It's over."

But the fellow had clearly been pushed beyond endurance. Eyes wild, the valet came at Trevor, fingers scratching, legs kicking out. Trevor ducked under the blows, landed a few himself, anything to keep the man back.

Cord coughed, bending over, and Trevor backed away. The valet's head came up, smile wicked, and he snatched up the knife and rushed at Trevor. There was no time, no place to escape. Trevor crossed his arms, prepared to take the blow.

"Dolly, attack!" Gwen shouted.

A wall of muscle slammed into Cord, knocking him flat. The knife skittered across the floor to fetch up against the far wall. Dolly set herself down on the valet's back, tongue lolling as if she were well satisfied with herself.

"Good girl," Gwen said as if quite satisfied, also. "Stay."

Trevor dropped his arms and went to retrieve the knife. It was done; Gwen was safe. Still the emotions rolled through him, and his fingers tightened on the handle of the blade.

"Mercy," Cord wheezed as Trevor approached.

Trevor gazed down at him, trapped under Dolly's bulk. He was a sick, tormented old man, driven mad by dreams of wealth. And Trevor might have been no different if it hadn't been for Gwen and Blackcliff.

Thank You, Lord. I still don't know why my father sent me here, but I am beginning to realize why You, my Father, did.

"God grants mercy," Trevor told the valet, "but I'm not sure the magistrates will be so lenient." He stepped around the valet and crossed to Gwen's side.

She smiled up at him as he started cutting free the ropes. He wanted to gather her in his arms, never let go. "Are you all right?" he asked.

She flexed her fingers as one arm came free. "Lovely, now that I know you and Dolly are fine." She lowered her voice and leaned closer to him, and the scent of roses was never sweeter. "Were you telling the truth? Are the jewels a humbug?"

"We may never know," he murmured, pausing to meet her concerned gaze. "But it isn't important, Gwen. All that matters is that I have you back safe."

The last of the ropes parted, and he drew her to her feet, cradling her close, allowing himself a slow, easy breath. She rested her head on his chest as if savoring the closeness, too.

Beside them, Cord moaned under Dolly's weight.

Trevor pulled back. "I'll have to take him to the constable, but I don't like leaving you."

She slipped her hand in his. "Then we'll take him together."

Her hand felt right in his; her smile lit the dim room. Trevor pressed a kiss against her knuckles. "Together, then. You deal with Dolly, and I'll deal with our thieving valet. But when we get back to the Hall, we must talk."

She sobered and nodded.

And so Trevor found himself at the tail of a somber procession through the village of Blackcliff. Gwen led the way, basket on one arm, hair tumbled down around her shoulders in a fiery cascade. Though she had Dolly's leash in her other hand, the mastiff walked just behind her, casting looks and the occasional growl back at John Cord. If he had been the one to attack Gwen's father, Trevor could understand why the dog might have more than one reason to have taken him in dislike.

Trevor and Cord came last, Trevor's hand firmly on the man's thin shoulder. Though Cord's hands were bound by the longest remaining pieces of the rope, he walked with his head high, his steps measured, as if above the village and its occupants even now.

People peered out of cottage windows, came hurrying from their gardens. Mrs. Billings, shaking out a dust cloth on the steps of the inn, paused to watch them approach the George. Trevor put on his haughtiest look, nose in the air the way he had dissuaded presumptuous students at school who wanted to know his background. It was sufficient to discourage anyone from following him now.

Casperson took Cord into custody, ambling around his counter to put his large hand on the valet's neck with a distasteful lift of his bulbous nose. "And what is he charged with, Sir Trevor?"

"Attempted murder, kidnapping, assault, theft and trespassing," Trevor replied. "It seems he was the one who attacked Mr. Allbridge after the assembly on Saturday."

Gwen beamed at him, clearly pleased he'd cleared her father so neatly.

"You're making a mistake," Cord protested, squirming in the constable's grip. "You need my help to find the jewels. I'm the only one the colonel trusted!"

Casperson held him at arm's length with a frown. "Jewels? What jewels?"

"A fortune!" Cord promised, holding up his bound hands. "Set me free, and I'll lead you to them."

Trevor clucked his tongue. "A shame. I fear his disease has driven him mad."

Casperson glanced at Trevor, then back at the valet as if uncertain who to believe.

"I've a bottle of horehound syrup right here," Gwen said, reaching into her basket. "I'll leave it for his use, Mr. Casperson."

The shopkeeper nodded, smile returning. "More syrup? Excellent news! We have all missed your mother's cures, Miss Allbridge."

He gave John Cord a little shake that made the valet stumble. "And I've a nice spot in the cellar to set this fellow until the next session of court. The magistrates will take a dim view of his behavior. I hope you have sufficient money to pay for your victuals while you wait, sir, or I fear you won't be getting many."

Cord blanched.

"Give him a warm bed," Trevor said. "And food and medicine as he needs them. Send the bills to Blackcliff."

The valet stared at him, but Gwen's smile only grew.

The constable scratched his ample gut. "You're a kinder man than I am, Sir Trevor. He's lucky you're the master of Blackcliff."

Trevor winked at Gwen. "Just trying to shepherd our little flock, Mr. Casperson."

Gwen gasped. Trevor frowned, but she quickly pressed her lips together as if hiding a secret. Then she turned to the constable.

"Do you need us for anything else, Mr. Casperson? I'd like to get home before Father worries."

He waved his free hand. "Of course, of course.

I know where to find you if I have questions." His booming laugh was nearly as loud as Dolly's bark.

"Thank you!" Gwen seized Trevor's hand and tugged him out of the shop.

"What happened?" he demanded as she steered him for the Hall, Dolly bounding ahead of them.

She glanced at him, dark gaze merry. "Oh, nothing terribly important. I think I know how to find the jewels!"

No matter how much Trevor begged, and he was quite endearing while pleading with his green eyes wide and eager, Gwen refused to explain until they reached Blackcliff. Then she left Dolly in Mrs. Bentley's care and hurried for the entryway.

"You mentioned being Blackcliff's shepherd," she said, bending over the statue. She struggled to lift it, but Trevor took the little shepherd easily from her grip. "And I remembered how this statue kept moving."

"Industrious fellow," Trevor agreed. "I'm assuming that was Cord, trying to make me think the house was haunted so I'd leave."

"Oh, Mr. Cord was moving him," Gwen replied, "but I think you mistake the colonel's purpose for the statue." She felt along the cold stone. What would it be: His staff? His arm? Her fingers glazed the wood enclosing the base, and her heart gave a leap. "The base! Of course!"

Trevor tipped the statue upside down and frowned

as he studied it. "It seems solid enough. I looked for hidden compartments earlier and found none."

"I don't think the jewels are in the statue. But isn't it strange that the base is the same shape as the medallions in the paneling, paneling that Colonel Umbrey had installed?"

His brows went up. "Do you think the statue is a key?"

She nodded with a grin. "Let's find out."

They started in the withdrawing room and worked their way through the house. Most rooms had a medallion in the center of each wall, depending on the placement of the windows, door and fireplace. The library with all its bookcases had none; the music room had three.

Yet each time Trevor inserted the base into the medallion, nothing happened. Gwen was certain she was right, but she could see Trevor's doubt by the growing frown on his handsome face. When they reached the top of the stairs to try the rooms on the chamber story, she caught his arm.

"Have faith! We'll find them. I know it."

"Faith." His smile reappeared. "I find that easier since coming to Blackcliff."

Gwen squeezed his arm, then released him. "The fells have that effect on people."

He moved to block her path. "*You* have that effect on people, Gwen. You're what's holding this village, this house together. Your love, your determination, humble me."

Warmth rushed up her body. "What a lovely thing to say! But we have a lot more rooms to try." She dodged around him. "Let's start in the sitting room. I always thought it was an odd place to put one, just at the top of the stairs and with no door to close off the draughts. Maybe that's why he had the chaise moved to the music room—he needed room for the jewels."

"Gwen," he protested, though she heard the sound of his boots against the carpet as he followed her. "I'm trying to tell you how much I admire you."

"And you know I admire you greatly, as well," she said, casting about for the medallion. The upstairs sitting room had a wide window overlooking the front of the house; it took up most of one wall and shed light on the grouping of chairs and tables the room boasted. The marble fireplace took up the east wall, and the arched opening by which they'd entered took up much of the south. The only medallion in the room was on the west wall.

"There!" She drew up beside it and waited for him to insert the base of the statue.

"This isn't important," he said, cradling the shepherd in his arms. "None of this is important—the jewels, this house, my baronetcy, if you aren't beside me."

Was he trying to propose? Oh, how she wanted him to propose! But if he proposed before finding the fortune, wouldn't he wonder whether he might have done better? Wouldn't he suspect that he had settled for a bargain bride?

Gwen dimpled up at him. "And I assure you I feel the same about you. Now connect the base."

He sighed. "You aren't listening."

"Not right now, but I will later, I promise."

He eyed her. "It isn't going to work."

"You don't know that," Gwen said, reaching over and swinging up the base, "until you try."

The base slipped into the medallion, just as it had in all the other rooms. Only this time, there was a very loud click.

Gwen froze, afraid even to look at Trevor. "Did you hear that?"

In answer, Trevor pressed the statue deeper.

"Turn it," Gwen said and was surprised to hear her voice come out in a whisper.

Trevor rotated the statue, and the medallion rotated with it. A vertical crack appeared in the paneling, separating a portion from the rest. Trevor pulled back, and a narrow section of wall swung open. They both peered inside.

The space was a honeycomb of crisscrossing shelves, all lined in black velvet. In each square lay a single gem. Trevor pushed the door wider, and the sunlight from the window glinted on the faceted surfaces. Rubies, sapphires and emeralds sparkled like the rainbow. Gwen caught her breath.

Trevor stared at them. He reached in a hand, hesitantly Gwen thought, and touched this one and that.

"There must be a least thirty of them," Gwen marveled.

"A fortune," Trevor agreed, and she could hear the awe in his voice as he pulled back his hand.

Joy bubbled up inside her, and she wrapped her arms about him and hugged him tight. "Oh, Trevor, you did it! You found your fortune! Blackcliff is saved!"

Chapter Twenty-Four

⚜

Trevor held Gwen close, gaze unable to move from the gems winking at him in the safe. If they were as valuable as he suspected, they'd bring him enough to set himself up in a prestigious London town house, purchase a traveling carriage, buy the finest clothes and live like an honorable gentleman. He could repair Blackcliff Mine, buy David Newton that organ, provide for the people of Blackcliff. The jewels could give him everything he'd ever wanted, once.

Now he wanted more.

He freed one arm from Gwen and swung shut the door.

"What are you doing?" she cried, disengaging from him.

He pulled the statue free. "There will be time enough later to sort them out. Right now, I have other things on my mind."

Her face clouded. "Of course. You have plans to make."

"We do indeed." He bent and set the little shepherd statue carefully on the floor at his feet.

The Lord is my shepherd; I shall not want.

You have given me the opportunity to fill every need, Lord.

He maketh me to lie down in green pastures.

Blackcliff may not have many pastures, but it is a good place, Lord.

He restoreth my soul.

You brought me back to You, Lord. Thank You.

The prayer passed in an instant, yet he felt it lingering as he straightened.

Gwen was watching him. "I've dreaded this moment," she murmured. "I can't watch you ride off for London." As if she feared she'd said too much, she stood taller, and her smile returned, teasing. "Dolly's grown very fond of Icarus."

Icarus! Who was still walking in front of the vicarage while Ruth Newton fended off all questions like a warrior queen. And then there was Gwen's father, preparing to rush to Carlisle. Trevor would have to explain, but first he had to tell Gwen everything.

He took her hand and cradled it in his own. Such a strong hand, a purposeful hand, yet one touch set him to yearning for a different life.

"And dare I hope," he murmured, "that you've become as fond of Icarus's master?"

"You know I have," she replied, but her smile was weak around the edges. "You will take a part of me with you when you leave."

He held her hand against his chest, wishing she could know how much his heart beat for her. "Then perhaps I'd better not leave."

She looked away. "But you must go. I understand that. You want to prove you can be the proper London gentleman. The opinions of Society are very important to you."

"True." But now God's opinion, her opinion, meant far more.

Her lower lip trembled, and she raised her chin. "I promised I'd be brave. I told myself I'd only ask you to save Blackcliff. I told the Lord you needed to find your own path. But, oh, Trevor, I don't want you to go."

He could not help the hope that rose inside him. "And what if I asked you to come with me as my wife?"

She stilled, gaping at him. His energetic, confident, determined love was finally speechless.

Trevor chuckled. "You needn't rush to answer. The next few minutes should suffice."

"You think I would make you wait?" She pulled her hand free and threw her arms around his neck. "You shall have your answer now, sir. Yes! Yes, I will marry you!"

Trevor bent and brushed his lips against hers, savoring the sweetness that was Gwen alone. She kissed him back, full of fire, full of joy. His life was about to change, for the better, for the best. He could hardly wait.

At length, he pulled back to gaze at her flushed face. "You're sure? No second thoughts?"

"None!" She was so happy he could not doubt her. "If you want to live in London, that's where we'll live." She glanced down at her cotton skirts. "Though, mind you, I'm not sure I'll do you credit during the Season. I have come to the realization that I shall never be perfect."

"Neither will I, but you do any man credit, in the Season or out, just as you are." Trevor gathered her close once more and rested his head atop her silky curls. "I don't plan to do more than visit London a few times a year in any event. Blackcliff will be our home."

"Oh, Trevor!" He could feel her relax against him as if he'd lifted the last burden. "But now I must ask you the same question," she murmured against his chest. "Are you sure?"

"Completely. What I want, I found here, with you. I promised God I'd go where He led, and Blackcliff is part of that plan. I'm sure of it." He gazed down at her, smoothing a curl back from her dear face. "I love you, Gwen."

Her look captured his heart. "And I love you. More than you can know."

Trevor held her, but he knew she was wrong. No one could mistake Gwen's love. It flowed from her touch, blossomed from her smile. With Gwen beside him, Blackcliff was no longer a house.

It was their home.

* * * * *

Dear Reader,

Thank you for choosing *An Honorable Gentleman*. Sir Trevor piqued my interest when he rode Icarus onto the page as Chase Dearborn's friend in *The Irresistible Earl*. I hope you enjoyed reading how he came to meet his match, and his Lord, among the natural wonders of Cumberland.

That area, the Lake District in England, is one of the country's most beautiful, with towering peaks and long lakes. The poet Wordsworth made his home there for many years. His "Guide to the Lakes" in 1810 drew hundreds of tourists to the area, and they continue to come today.

I welcome visitors to my website, too. Please feel free to contact me via www.reginascott.com, where you can also read about my upcoming books. Blessings!

Regina Scott

Questions for Discussion

1. Sir Trevor Fitzwilliam is disappointed with his new estate when he first arrives. Have you ever been disappointed in a gift? How did you react to the giver?

2. Gwen Allbridge is afraid of taking her mother's place in the village. Have you had to follow a parent or sibling you thought was more talented? How did you handle it?

3. Many of the villagers depend on the Blackcliff estate for their livelihood. What industries does your town depend on? How does your town react when one of its industries does poorly?

4. Gwen struggles with the idea of leaving Blackcliff. What kinds of things pull us away from our childhood homes? How can we go about making a new place home?

5. Sir Trevor is amazed by what he learns in the Bible. What story in the Bible is your favorite? Where did you first hear it? How did you react to it?

6. Gwen is devoted to her family, including her dog, Dolly. Do you or someone you know have a beloved pet? How is it part of the family?

7. John Cord feels that his previous employer owes him more than wages for his hard work and sacrifice. What do Christians owe those who serve today?

8. Horace Allbridge uses alcohol to dull the pain from his wife's death. What other things do people use to avoid painful memories? How can we help those who mourn?

9. Gwen sees God's provision in His wondrous works. Where do you most often see the Father's hand?

10. Trevor blames God for his difficult upbringing. Why are some people raised in more difficult surroundings than others? How can such trials shape us?

11. Gwen tries to order her world through hard work. At what point should we turn to God and let Him take the burden?

INSPIRATIONAL

Wholesome romances that touch the heart and soul.

Love Inspired.
HISTORICAL

COMING NEXT MONTH
AVAILABLE DECEMBER 6, 2011

MAIL-ORDER CHRISTMAS BRIDES
Jillian Hart and Janet Tronstad

THE CAPTAIN'S CHRISTMAS FAMILY
Glass Slipper Brides
Deborah Hale

THE EARL'S MISTAKEN BRIDE
The Parson's Daughters
Abby Gaines

HER REBEL HEART
Shannon Farrington

REQUEST YOUR FREE BOOKS!

2 FREE INSPIRATIONAL NOVELS
PLUS 2
FREE
MYSTERY GIFTS

Love Inspired
HISTORICAL
INSPIRATIONAL HISTORICAL ROMANCE

YES! Please send me 2 FREE Love Inspired® Historical novels and my 2 FREE mystery gifts (gifts are worth about $10). After receiving them, if I don't wish to receive any more books, I can return the shipping statement marked "cancel." If I don't cancel, I will receive 4 brand-new novels every month and be billed just $4.49 per book in the U.S. or $4.99 per book in Canada. That's a saving of at least 22% off the cover price. It's quite a bargain! Shipping and handling is just 50¢ per book in the U.S. and 75¢ per book in Canada.* I understand that accepting the 2 free books and gifts places me under no obligation to buy anything. I can always return a shipment and cancel at any time. Even if I never buy another book, the two free books and gifts are mine to keep forever.

102/302 IDN FEHF

Name	(PLEASE PRINT)	
Address		Apt. #
City	State/Prov.	Zip/Postal Code

Signature (if under 18, a parent or guardian must sign)

Mail to the **Reader Service:**
IN U.S.A.: P.O. Box 1867, Buffalo, NY 14240-1867
IN CANADA: P.O. Box 609, Fort Erie, Ontario L2A 5X3

Not valid for current subscribers to Love Inspired Historical books.

Want to try two free books from another series?
Call 1-800-873-8635 or visit www.ReaderService.com.

* Terms and prices subject to change without notice. Prices do not include applicable taxes. Sales tax applicable in N.Y. Canadian residents will be charged applicable taxes. Offer not valid in Quebec. This offer is limited to one order per household. All orders subject to credit approval. Credit or debit balances in a customer's account(s) may be offset by any other outstanding balance owed by or to the customer. Please allow 4 to 6 weeks for delivery. Offer available while quantities last.

Your Privacy—The Reader Service is committed to protecting your privacy. Our Privacy Policy is available online at www.ReaderService.com or upon request from the Reader Service.

We make a portion of our mailing list available to reputable third parties that offer products we believe may interest you. If you prefer that we not exchange your name with third parties, or if you wish to clarify or modify your communication preferences, please visit us at www.ReaderService.com/consumerschoice or write to us at Reader Service Preference Service, P.O. Box 9062, Buffalo, NY 14269. Include your complete name and address.

LIHI1B

When former Amishman Gideon Troyer sees his Amish ex-girlfriend on television at a quilt auction to raise money for surgery to correct her blindness, he's stunned and feels a pull drawing him back to his past.

Read on for a sneak preview of
THE CHRISTMAS QUILT
by Patricia Davids.

Rebecca Beachy pulled the collar of her coat closed against a cold gust of wind and ugly memories. An early storm was on its way, but God had seen fit to hold it off until the quilt auction was over. For that, she was thankful.

When she and her aunt finally reached their seats, Rebecca unbuttoned her coat and removed her heavy bonnet. Many of the people around her greeted her in her native Pennsylvania Dutch. Leaning closer to her aunt, she asked, "Is my *kapp* on straight? Do I look okay?"

"And why wouldn't you look okay?" Vera asked.

"Because I may have egg yolk from breakfast on my dress, or my back may be covered with dust from the buggy seat. I don't know. Just tell me I look presentable." She knew everyone would be staring at her when her quilt was brought up for auction. She didn't like being the center of attention.

"You look lovely." The harsh whisper startled her.

She turned her face toward the sound coming from behind her and caught the scent of a man's spicy aftershave. The voice must belong to an *Englisch* fellow. *"Danki."*

"You're most welcome." He coughed, and she realized he was sick.

"You sound as if you should be abed with that cold."

"So I've been told," he admitted.

"It is a foolish fellow who doesn't follow *goot* advice.

"Some people definitely consider me foolish." His raspy voice held a hint of amusement.

He was poking fun at himself. She liked that. There was something familiar about him, but she couldn't put her finger on what it was. "Have we met?"

To see if Rebecca and Gideon can let go of the past
and move forward to a future together, pick up
THE CHRISTMAS QUILT by Patricia Davids
Available in December
from Love Inspired Books.